SAMARA SHANKER

Atheneum Books for Young Readers

atheneum   NEW YORK LONDON TORONTO SYDNEY NEW DELHI

aktheneum

ATHENEUM BOOKS FOR YOUNG READERS
An imprint of Simon & Schuster Children's Publishing Division
1230 Avenue of the Americas, New York, New York 10020

Text © 2022 by Samara Shanker
Jacket illustration © 2022 by Shane Cluskey
Jacket design by Greg Stadnyk © 2022 by Simon & Schuster, Inc.
Interior illustration © 2022 by Shane Cluskey

For information about special discounts for bulk purchases, please contact Simon & Schuster Special Sales at 1-866-506-1949 or business@simonandschuster.com.
The Simon & Schuster Speakers Bureau can bring authors to your live event. For more information or to book an event, contact the Simon & Schuster Speakers Bureau at 1-866-248-3049 or visit our website at www.simonspeakers.com.
Interior design by Irene Metaxatos
The text for this book was set in ITC Bookman Std.
The illustrations for this book were rendered digitally.
Manufactured in the United States of America
0722 FFG
First Edition
10 9 8 7 6 5 4 3 2 1
Library of Congress Cataloging-in-Publication Data
Names: Shanker, Samara, author.
Title: Naomi Teitelbaum ends the world / Samara Shanker.
Description: First edition. | New York : Atheneum Books for Young Readers, [2022] | Audience: Ages 8-12. | Summary: Almost-thirteen-year-old Naomi receives a mysterious package containing a tiny clay Golem that obeys her every command, and she is unprepared for the chaos he creates when she sends him away with instructions to save the world.
Identifiers: LCCN 2021046046 | ISBN 9781665905022 (hardcover) | ISBN 9781665905046 (ebook)
Subjects: CYAC: Golem—Fiction. | Helpfulness—Fiction. | Responsibility—Fiction. | Jews—United States—Fiction. | Los Angeles (Calif.)—Fiction. | LCGFT: Novels.
Classification: LCC PZ7.1.S4818 Nao 2022 | DDC [Fic]—dc23
LC record available at https://lccn.loc.gov/2021046046

For Nate and Charlie.
May your lives be full of adventure
and friendship,
and may there always be someone
to cut the tags out of your clothes.

1

A MYSTERIOUS PACKAGE

The box was addressed to *Ms. Naomi Teitelbaum*, which made Naomi feel very grown-up. It came in the same batch of mail as a check for thirty-six dollars from Naomi's aunt Rachel, who was in Prague for the winter on a research trip, and a card from Naomi's great-uncle Irving, who was too old to fly from Florida to California by himself. Naomi's Bat Mitzvah was three weeks away, and the mail was practically all Bat Mitzvah related: gifts, late RSVPs, decorations for the party. It wasn't that strange, then, that the box came addressed to Naomi. It *was* a little strange that there was no return address indicating who the box was from, but that happened from time to time when her older relatives sent things. Naomi stared at the dark, reddish-brown wrapping paper while her mom sorted through the rest of the boring mail.

"Can I open it now?" she asked.

"Hmm?" Her mom looked up and raised an eyebrow. "Not right now. Whatever it is will keep until after your lesson with the rabbi." She checked her watch and frowned. "Speaking of which, why aren't you ready to go?"

"I'm ready!" Naomi lifted her foot up over the counter so her mom could see that she was wearing shoes. "I'm so ready. I'm so super-duper ready, I could open this package right now and not even be late!"

"Where are your headphones?"

Naomi squinted. "I don't need headphones to meet with Rabbi Levinson."

Mom squinted right back. "You need your headphones if you're going to practice your Torah portion in the car."

Naomi groaned. "This is an *injustice*."

"Don't try that with me, Naomi Sarah. I've

been dealing in fancy words longer than you've been alive."

"Yeah, but you work for The *Establishment*."

Mom didn't dignify that with a response. She sent a meaningful look at Naomi's Bat Mitzvah binder. "Ugh, *Mom*." Naomi threw herself sideways over the counter. "I practiced my prayers already today, and Mama said I only had to do that."

Her mom's other eyebrow rose to meet the first one, high on her forehead. She put the mail down, her shiny, white-tipped nails clicking against the counter. "Is that so?" Naomi nodded quickly. "Hmm," her mom said. "So if I call your mama right now, she'll back you up?"

"We-*ell*, she'll definitely back me up that I did my prayers," Naomi told her.

"That, young lady, is not the same thing."

Naomi scowled and stomped over to the couch. She knew she had been defeated, but she wasn't going down without a fight. "I know my Torah portion, Mom," she whined, trying to tug her headphones out from where they had tangled in the couch cushions. They were caught on something, and she had to give them a good hard yank to try to get them loose. "Cantor Debbie said I was just about ready."

"'Just about' isn't the same as 'completely,'" Mom said. She was always saying things like that. Naomi's mom was an assistant district attorney for Los Angeles County and a total perfectionist. Naomi and her older sister, Deena, were always getting lectures about paying attention to details and keeping track of their work. Naomi's messy backpack made her mom sigh more times a day than anything Deena ever did.

"Fine," Naomi said. Her headphones came free after another sharp tug, and she stomped her way back over to the counter to get her phone. "*Now* I'm ready."

Her mom's phone started ringing just then, and she waved Naomi off toward the front door. As she gathered her purse and her cardigan with one hand, she lifted the phone to her ear with the other and said in her professional lawyer voice, "Rebecca Teitelbaum."

"*Rebecca Teitelbaum,*" Naomi mimicked, trying to make her voice sound like her mom's. It was hard—she could never get her vowels to sound round enough. Naomi's mama didn't have a different phone voice; she just used her normal voice all the time. Though Naomi supposed that her mama didn't need a special voice to be a yoga instructor. She didn't even answer the phone like Mom did, with her whole name: *Miriam Teitelbaum.* She usually just said, *Hello,* or, if it was Naomi or Deena calling, *How did you get this number?* That had stopped being funny after the fourth or fifth time she did it, but she still answered the phone that way, almost every time. Deena was seventeen now and did a lot of eye-rolling at their mama.

Naomi climbed into the back seat of the car with her Bat Mitzvah binder and hit play on her phone, ignoring Deena, who slid into the front seat and made a face at her. Naomi guessed Mom was dropping Deena off at the mall or something. She waved her phone at her sister to show she was listening to her recording and couldn't talk to Deena about whatever random pop star she was obsessed with that day.

Cantor Debbie's voice chanted the Hebrew words while Naomi followed along quietly, trying not to disturb her mom on the phone. At the end of the recording, Cantor Debbie explained what the Torah portion meant and which words were special. Naomi had listened to the recording so many times that she could practically recite the explanation along with Cantor Debbie. *"And when God calls out to Moses from the burning bush, Moses responds 'hineni,' here I am. This is more than just saying that he's physically there. When Moses says 'hineni,' he is saying that he is present before God and committed to listening and taking on the duties that he is asked to,"* Naomi recited along with the recording. "Whatever that means." She threw her arm across her eyes and sighed, long and pained, forgetting for a minute that she was trying to be quiet. In the driver's seat, her mom snapped her fingers. Universal mom-speak for, *Be quiet. I'm on the phone.* Deena turned around in the passenger seat and snapped her fingers too, just to be obnoxious. Naomi bared her teeth at her.

"Do your work!" Deena hissed.

"Mind your business!" Naomi growled back.

Mom snapped her fingers again, and both of them rolled their eyes. Deena turned back around. Naomi pulled her feet up on the car seat and watched the street signs pass by as Cantor

Debbie chanted her way through the prayers for after-the-Torah portion.

The car pulled up to the temple. Naomi swung the door open as quietly as she could so Mom wouldn't shush her again, blew her a kiss, stuck her tongue out at her sister, and hurried inside. Mom had dropped her at the side entrance, which led right to Rabbi Levinson's office. He was at his desk, the office door wide open and the giant beanbag chair that covered the half of Rabbi Levinson's office that wasn't behind his desk—a gift from the class a year ahead of Deena—freshly vacuumed and waiting for his next student. He looked up and waved as Naomi scooched her way inside and clambered up onto the beanbag.

"How are you today, Naomi?" Rabbi Levinson asked.

Naomi shrugged. "Fine. I like your yarmulke."

Rabbi Levinson patted the blue and green tie-dyed yarmulke that sat perched on his hair and smiled. It made him look very young. Well, not *young* young, but much younger than Naomi's moms, at least. Rabbi Levinson was in that puzzling grown-up age bracket that Naomi's best friend Becca Reznik liked to call "preparental" in the same slightly condescending tone Mrs. Reznik said "prepubescent."

Naomi had known the rabbi since she was in kindergarten, and he had seemed old and wise when she was five, but now that she was about to be thirteen and was allowed to hear some of the gossip, she often heard her moms describe the rabbi to their friends as "Dave—you know, the cute young rabbi at Beth Torah," which was weird and gross. She also knew that Deena and all her friends had crushes on him, which was weirder and grosser. Rabbi Levinson wasn't revolting, Naomi figured, eyeing him critically across the desk as he pulled out whatever book they would be discussing that day and his copy of Naomi's Bat Mitzvah speech. His hair was stylish and fluffy under his colorful yarmulke, and his glasses were cool and trendy without being hipster. He was tall and smiley, and Naomi knew he worked out because she saw him running by their house once in a while, but he was *old.*

Anyway, you couldn't have a crush on a rabbi. Naomi's Hebrew school teacher had explained that Judaism didn't really approach sin the same way other religions did, but Naomi was reasonably sure that it was probably considered a sin to have a crush on a rabbi. If it wouldn't be completely mortifying, she'd ask Cantor Debbie about it. As it was, Naomi just fidgeted as Rabbi Levinson held out his hand for her Bat Mitzvah binder.

She passed it over. "I've been working on my speech."

The rabbi nodded encouragingly. "That's good! What kind of stuff have you been thinking about?"

Naomi drummed her fingers on the desk. "Well, Cantor Debbie says that the story is about taking responsibility."

"Sure."

"But Moses didn't really cause any of the stuff that happened, right? He was just . . . born at the wrong time and things got put on him."

"Sure," the rabbi said again. He never disagreed with his students, Naomi had learned. He just asked gentle questions until they figured out what he was aiming for.

"So, then, why is it Moses's responsibility to go free the slaves? Just because God asked him to? That doesn't seem fair."

"What do you think would be fair?"

"I don't know! Couldn't God have just taken care of it?"

Rabbi Levinson nodded. "Maybe. So why do you think he asked Moses?"

"That's what I'm asking you!" Naomi exclaimed. That got her a laugh.

"No, that's what I'm asking *you*," said Rabbi Levinson.

Naomi huffed. "Maybe God was just lazy."

"Naomi."

"Sorry," she muttered. She tapped her fingers on the desk again and took a candy from the bowl on the rabbi's desk. The rabbi let her think, watching her fidget with a small smile. Finally, Naomi tucked the candy into her cheek and frowned, trying to remember all the discussions she'd had with the rabbi and Cantor Debbie over the last few months. "Maybe because slavery is a problem between humans, and it wouldn't be fair or helpful if God just fixed it, because no one would actually learn anything. Like the Pharaoh would never see that he had been wrong and that there were consequences for that."

"What an excellent point!" Rabbi Levinson said. "So, by using Moses as his messenger, God is helping his people learn to face their own mistakes and fix the things that are wrong, instead of relying only on miracles."

"But they did rely on miracles!" Naomi protested. "At the end, Pharaoh changed his mind and they had to part the sea! And anyway, Pharaoh only let them go in the first place because of the plagues."

Rabbi Levinson leaned his elbows on the desk. "Hmm. That's true. So why did God even bother trying to get Moses to solve it?"

"Well, you have to *try*!"

Rabbi Levinson smiled, and Naomi groaned. "All right, fine," she said. "But still, why Moses?"

"Why not?"

"He'd already left!"

"Did he feel good about the way he left?"

"Probably not."

"So maybe Moses felt he had to try, too." The rabbi let her take another candy, then pulled the bowl out of her reach. "I don't want your moms calling me about you coming home with a sugar high," he joked. Then he went on. "What Cantor Debbie told you about taking responsibility is true. The word 'hineni' shows up a few times in the Torah, usually when people are being called to do things that seem unfair, or at least very, very difficult. Did Cantor Debbie tell you what 'hineni' means?"

"It means 'here I am,'" Naomi told him.

"Here I am," Rabbi Levinson echoed. "God calls to Moses, and Moses shows up. He's ready. He doesn't say, 'Who's going to deal with this?' He says, 'I'm here. I'll deal with it.'"

Naomi nodded, and the rabbi nodded back. "Now, did you read the passage I sent you? I think you're going to find it really interesting."

Naomi's mom picked her up—without Deena this time—and took her home. She was on another call, so Naomi fidgeted in silence the whole way, thinking a little about what the rabbi had told her about her Torah portion but mostly thinking about opening her present. Mom nodded when Naomi pointed to it when they got home, and Naomi raced to drop her shoes in the rack by the door, then skidded on her sock feet over to the counter. She dumped her Bat Mitzvah binder, grabbed the box and the sparkly pink envelope that was probably from her cousin Laney, blew a kiss at her distracted mom, and ran down the hall to her room. She video-called her other best friend, Eitan, as soon as she was in there, propping the phone up on her pillow so he could see her sitting cross-legged on her bed.

Eitan's enthusiastic round face appeared on-screen almost immediately. "Nae-Nae! My best friend in the whole world who also has excellent timing! I just got home from my lesson with Cantor Debbie. What are you doing?"

"Ugh," Naomi said, falling sideways dramatically. "I just got home from my meeting with the rabbi. Guess we just missed each other at temple. *And* my mom made me practice my prayers in the car. It's like having *homework*."

Eitan clicked his tongue sympathetically. "Homework the very first day after school lets out. It's what we get for having winter birthdays. No winter break when there's a Bar Mitzvah on the horizon. Or a Bat Mitzvah," he added at Naomi's scowl. She nodded, satisfied. She'd been reminding Eitan a lot recently about the dangers of defaulting to male language. It helped that his mom backed Naomi up whenever she overheard them. He flopped down onto his couch, and his picture on the phone shook for a moment. "But think of the presents," he said wistfully.

"And the party!" Naomi added. "And the food!"

"And the presents!" Eitan said again. "You really can't forget the presents."

"Mama would say we're disregarding the religious and communal significance of the ceremony." Naomi sighed. In fact, her mama *had* said that—many times. Mama talked a lot about "raising them to be citizens of the world."

"Your mama has a lot of things to say about the rampant consumerism of the youth," Eitan said dolefully, "but I just want enough Bar Mitzvah money to pay for space camp."

"They're only going to give you bonds that your parents can put into college savings," Naomi reminded him. "And, anyway, we're buying into the capitalist lies that we could be rich if we save up enough," she told him, parroting her mama's favorite news show host.

"You live in a McMansion in the Valley, Nae," Eitan reminded her. Naomi shrugged. She didn't control where she lived. Eitan rolled his eyes. "Whatever. I got thirty-six dollars from Uncle Jeff today. That's a start."

"Oh, me too! From Aunt Rachel."

"Double chai," they chorused, with little enough sarcasm that neither of their respective parents would scold them for it.

"What happened to scorning capitalist values?" Eitan joked.

"I still have to live in a society, Eitan," Naomi said. "Anyway, that's why I called you! Presents! There's a new mystery present!"

Eitan gave an exaggerated sigh. "Old people on the internet."

"I know, right?" Naomi snorted. "Mom said I could open it. Want to help me guess who it's from?"

"You know I do." Eitan leaned close to the phone, and Naomi giggled at his distorted picture. "Shut up," he said. "I need to see."

"You could just come over," she reminded him.

"Will you wait for me to open it?"

"No."

"Then I'm going to stay right here, thank you very much." He did lean back far enough that his nose stopped looking squished against the camera, though. "Open it, Nae."

Naomi tore the reddish-brown paper off the

package to reveal a perfectly white, square box. It wasn't the usual flimsy cardboard. Naomi wasn't entirely sure what it was made of. She lifted it to show Eitan, who didn't know what it was, either. "But what's *in* the box?" he demanded.

"I'm getting there!" It took her a moment to find the seam of the lid, but when she did, it came off fairly easily in her hands. She pushed aside the soft packing paper until her fingers brushed against something hard and rough. Her hand closed around it, and she lifted the item free. "Huh."

On-screen, Eitan was squinting at it. "It's a . . . figurine?"

"I'm not sure." Naomi turned the little clay figure around in her hands. It was the same reddish-brown color as the wrapping paper. It looked like someone had carved a tiny man out of clay. Its features were rough, just enough detail to see that it did have eyes and a mouth— little scoops out of the clay of its face that some- how still gave the impression of delicate work. It looked almost human but not close enough to be uncanny. She held it up and wiggled it at Eitan. "What a weird gift."

"Is there a note?"

Naomi dug through the box again until she found the tightly rolled scroll nestled in the tissue paper. A silver wax seal held it closed, and Naomi had to dig her nails into it until it broke. Across the top, in neat typewriter text, it said plainly: *For Naomi. To help.* Then there was some Hebrew that Naomi couldn't quite parse. It was the loopy, cursive kind with no vowels. She could barely pick out any of the letters. Underneath that, almost as incomprehensible with how embellished the script was, were the words *I Create as I Speak.* Below that was a blank line for a signature. There was a thin, perforated section along the bottom that had the same Hebrew words and instructions that read: *Place smaller scroll in Golem's head after completing signature of ownership.*

There was nothing else.

2

NAOMI WINS
A BET

Naomi didn't do anything with the little clay man—the Golem—until she got to Eitan's house the next day. She had promised both Eitan and Becca she'd wait to investigate it more until they were together. Eitan's dad picked her and Becca up in one fell swoop and dropped them both off on the driveway of his house before he headed to work. Naomi and Becca scrambled out of the car with their backpacks, and Mr. Snyder rolled down the passenger window to yell after them, "There are snacks in the fridge! Everyone has to eat at least one piece of fruit today."

They started walking backward down the driveway as he talked. "Okay," Becca called back. "Thanks, Mr. Snyder!"

"Eitan's mom will be home by five. Don't just watch TV!"

"We won't!" Naomi promised, and then they turned around and dashed toward the side door as Mr. Snyder drove away in the direction of the law office where he worked. Becca keyed in the door code, and she and Naomi tumbled through into the Snyders' pristine sitting room. Mrs. Snyder had done the whole house in shades of cream and beige, which meant that they had to be extra careful when they hung out at Eitan's house. Naomi liked going to Becca's house much better. There were four kids in the Reznik family—Becca was the oldest—and the closest to pristine their house ever got was organized chaos. But Eitan's house was closer to the arcade and to the mini golf course they were allowed to walk to if they wanted and had the added benefit of no little siblings running around trying to make Becca and her friends help with their dolls. Naomi had her own weird little doll to worry about.

She trooped with Becca up to Eitan's room. It

was only nine a.m., so they weren't surprised to find Eitan still in bed. Naomi's friend was many things—a chess genius, a baking mastermind, a good sport about Naomi's quest to rid him of his gender bias—but he was not an early riser. Becca whooped and threw herself heavily onto Eitan's bed, bouncing up and down on the mattress until he was grumbling and trying to shove her off. Naomi snorted and dropped onto the bed on his other side, shoving at him until there was enough room for her to sit against the headboard without being knocked off by Becca's antics.

"Who let you two miscreants into my house?" Eitan groaned, his words coming out muffled and a little jumbled together, like he was trying to talk without actually opening his mouth.

"We have a key code," Naomi told him primly.

"Plus, your dad came and got us *ages* ago," said Becca, scrubbing her hand over Eitan's head. It looked like his mom had just cut his hair, and Becca delighted in rubbing her hands over the fuzzy softness of his buzz cut. Eitan growled at her. She ignored it. "I'm serious. He was *early*. My mom made me wake up at *eight*."

"Disgusting." Eitan's syllables were starting to

sound less slurred together. That was a good sign. It meant he was almost awake enough for them to try to actually get him out of his bed.

Naomi snatched a pillow from him as he tried to put it over his head. "Nope," she told him. "We're here now. Get up!" She bounced a little like Becca had, and Eitan swatted blindly at her from inside his cocoon of blankets. She caught his hand and set a timer on his watch for fifteen minutes.

"When this timer goes off," she warned him, "we're coming back in. So you better be dressed and ready."

With that, Naomi and Becca hopped off the bed and marched together back down the stairs, Becca shouting behind them, "I brought toaster pastries!"

Exactly fifteen minutes later, a slightly rumpled Eitan came into the kitchen and threw himself over a barstool at the counter. He held his hand out wordlessly, and Becca slapped a silver-wrapped packet of toaster pastry into it. Eitan tore it open and took a bite, then ripped open the icing packet and squirted the contents directly into his mouth. Naomi wrinkled her nose.

"Gross."

"You're gross."

"Your face is gross."

"Your mom is gross."

"Which one?"

That pulled him up short, and Becca snorted, tossing her long, light-brown braid over her shoulder like she had been the one to win the argument. "Foiled again by the combined power of two Teitelbaum mothers. Anyway, are you human enough yet that we can check out Naomi's mystery present? Or do you need to destroy another prepackaged pastry?"

Eitan gave this some thought as he finished chewing. "I need another pastry," he decided. Becca gave him one, and he devoured it in the same way—Naomi mimed throwing up, and he threw the wrapper at her. Finally, he drank a glass of milk in three large gulps and said, "All right, let's see it."

The three of them gathered around the tasteful white coffee table in the living room, and Naomi produced the box. Becca and Eitan were silent as she unpacked the little clay Golem and set it gently on the table along with the scroll and its mystifying instructions. They passed both things around, each of them taking their time inspecting the Golem and then the paper. Then Becca placed them both back onto the table and looked up at Naomi. "So, do it."

Naomi blinked at her. "Do what?"

"Follow the instructions. Sign the scroll and put the little paper into the Golem's head."

"How do I even do that?"

Eitan pointed. "There's a seam, right around its head. I bet there's a way to open it."

"Like the box," Naomi said.

"Huh?"

"The box," she explained, holding up the package so Becca could inspect it. "It looked sealed like that too, but it had that little seam that opened up when I pushed in the right place."

"Cool," Becca said. "Make it happen, Nae."

Naomi felt worry pool in her stomach. She wasn't sure why she felt nervous about following the instructions, but her instincts were telling her it was more serious than they thought. She looked to Eitan. "What do you think?"

He shrugged. "I don't think anything. In all the

stories, you have to have a rabbi or a high priest or something to make a Golem turn on, so even if it is real, you won't be able to wake it up. Just do it. What's the worst that could happen?"

Both Becca and Naomi groaned. "Famous last words!" Naomi said accusingly. "You've cursed us!"

"Curses aren't real!" Eitan protested. "And I'm telling you, it won't work! Didn't either of you ever pay attention when Miss Shoshanna read us stories in Hebrew school?" Both girls stared at him, and Eitan sighed. "You're the worst. Whatever. I'm telling you nothing's going to happen. I'll bet you the thirty-six dollars I just got that nothing happens when you put the scroll in its head. It's just a weird toy one of your moms' cousins sent."

The words made a chill crawl up Naomi's spine, but she forced herself to ignore it. "You're right," she decided. "But if you're not, I'm definitely collecting on that bet. You're not the only one trying to save up for something. I need new worms for my compost bin, and Mom says she's done buying them."

"Gross." Eitan wrinkled his nose.

"Enough stalling!" Becca said. "Wake up the tiny magic man."

"No one's waking up," Eitan grumbled. Naomi stayed silent, but she took the pen Becca handed her and signed her name as neatly as she could on the scroll. Then she tore off the tiny strip at the bottom, careful not to rip it, and rolled it up tightly. She ended up with a nub of paper slightly smaller than the nail on her pinkie finger, which she handed to Eitan while she inspected the little Golem. There was a seam around its head, just as Eitan had said. As though someone had sliced the top off its skull like a watermelon and then glued it back together. Naomi pressed gently right at the center of its forehead, and the top of its head swung open, revealing a space just large enough for an object about the size of Naomi's pinkie fingernail. She reached out with a slightly unsteady hand, and Eitan dropped the paper into her palm. Very, very slowly, Naomi slid the paper into the space in the Golem's head. It fit exactly. As soon as she let go, the Golem's head swung closed.

They waited for about ten seconds, none of them daring to breathe. Nothing happened. Eitan snorted and sat back. "Told you."

Becca let out a disappointed sigh. "Man, I was hoping it would do something cool."

Naomi nodded, though she didn't think what she was feeling was disappointment, exactly. She might have almost said she was feeling relieved, but that didn't make any sense. She knew it would have been totally cool if the Golem had actually woken up, but that didn't stop her breath from coming a little easier anyway. Then, just as she was starting to relax, the Golem twitched in her hand.

Naomi screamed and dropped it, scrambling backward away from the coffee table. Becca and Eitan looked at her like she was crazy, but she pointed a shaky finger at the Golem. It had landed on the soft white carpet, no worse for the fall, dark against the bright clean rug. It was also moving. They watched, frozen, as the little statue twitched again, then wiggled its arms and legs in the air like a struggling bug. Then it sat up, the movements stiff and creaky, and turned its head side to side like it was looking for something.

The Golem's sightless gaze landed on Naomi. The shadows in its eyes were darker, like the little dents in the clay had gotten deeper, somehow. It still looked like an undecorated gingerbread man, but there was a new energy to the little statue that made it seem very, very alive. The Golem stood on stiff, jointless legs and began to move in a jerky, uneven gait across the carpet toward her. Naomi pressed back against the couch, watching as the Golem climbed up the arm of the couch and across the expanse of cushions until it stood in front of her, the expressionless clay face still somehow giving off a sense of expectation.

"What?" Naomi said. The Golem stayed silent, and Naomi immediately felt silly. Of course it didn't talk. It barely had a mouth. Though she would have also sworn until thirty seconds ago that it wouldn't wake up and follow her across the room, so maybe it wasn't *that* silly.

"What does it want?" Becca hissed, shoving at Naomi's shoulder. "Nae, do something!"

"Like what?" Naomi hissed back.

"Give it a task," Eitan whispered. "Golems need tasks."

Naomi took a breath, trying to force her completely blank mind to think of something she needed help with. Her mouth felt dry. A thought occurred to her. "Um"—she waved her hand vaguely at the Golem—"will you get me my water bottle from my backpack? Um . . . please? It's the black one." For a moment, the Golem just looked at her. Then it turned around and made its way back over the couch cushions and down to the carpet, where it trundled along until it was out of sight around the doorway to the kitchen. Naomi strained to hear the sound of tiny clay feet tapping across the tile, but the room was silent except for Eitan's excited breathing and the soft clicking sound Becca made with her tongue when she got anxious. Naomi was about to get up to go look for it when they heard what sounded a lot like stainless steel being dragged over tile—shockingly loud in the quiet house—and then the little Golem was back, resolutely pulling Naomi's scratched, sticker-covered metal water bottle behind it. It stopped by her feet and looked up at her expectantly. Hesitantly, Naomi reached down and took the bottle from it. "Thank you," she whispered.

Becca let out a whooshing breath. "Who sent you that?"

"I don't know," Naomi said. "There was no note. Maybe my mom knows." She prodded gently at the little figure. It was completely still once more. If it weren't for the strange new feeling that it was *alive* somehow, Naomi might have believed that it had never moved at all. Beside her, Eitan reached into his pocket and pulled out his wallet. He produced a small stack of crisp clean bills—thirty-six dollars from his uncle Jeff—and handed it to Naomi without a word.

3

TEENY-TINY
TROUBLES

Becca and Eitan, after they had gotten over their
initial shock, had both insisted that they should
find out more about the Golem if they could. If
nothing else, someone out there had access to
magic they hadn't thought was real until that
afternoon. As Eitan had said, it would be *epic* to
team up with them. Naomi wasn't as convinced
that finding someone with real magic would
actually be as epic as Eitan believed. Still, her
friends were right that more information would
only be a good thing, so the first thing she did
when she got home from Eitan's house was ask

her mom where the package had come from.

"Hmm?" Her mom looked up from her work laptop, her nails tapping against the stack of files next to her. "The gift in the red box? What was it?"

Naomi pulled the Golem out of her jacket pocket—she had given it very strict instructions to stay still while she talked to her mom—and held it out. Her mom took it, turning it over in her hands while Naomi held her breath and prayed that the Golem was as good of a listener as it seemed. Finally, her mom handed it back, and Naomi stowed it quickly in her pocket. "Did anyone mention it to you?" Naomi asked.

"No," her mom said. "It's an odd little gift, isn't it? There was no note?"

Naomi thought about the strange note with the words to activate the Golem on it and decided that that probably wasn't what her mom meant. "Just one of those preprinted ones that said who it was for," she lied.

"And no tag or anything in the box? We could call the company that shipped it and see if they have the name of the person who ordered it."

"There was nothing," Naomi told her.

Her mom let out a big sigh. "Some of your

relatives . . . I swear. It's like the Stone Age for them." Her computer *ding*ed and she turned back to it, opening up a new email with a worried look. "I have to get back to this, sorry, Nomes. Don't worry about the gift. If someone gets in touch with us about it, you'll write them a thank-you card then."

Naomi wasn't sure if she felt relieved or disappointed that there was no way to track down the sender. Either way, her stomach felt full of knots. She scooted closer for a second, pressing her face against her mom's shoulder and receiving a kiss on the top of her head for her trouble. "Okay, thanks, Mom," she said.

Her mom nodded absently, eyes back on the screen. She always worked from home on school breaks, since Naomi's mama couldn't exactly bring the yoga studio home. "Of course, hon. Do me a favor and see what Deens wants for dinner, okay?"

"Sure." Naomi left the kitchen and trudged up the stairs toward her sister's room, her hand wrapped tightly around the little figure in her pocket.

. . .

Two days after the Golem woke up, Naomi was beginning to get used to having the little clay figure following her around like a tiny, helpful shadow. What was harder to get used to was the fact that ever since the Golem woke up, Naomi had started *hallucinating*. At least, she hoped she was hallucinating. Though a practical voice in her head that sounded a lot like Eitan told her she wasn't. She was *seeing* things and hearing voices in her mind that got louder the closer she got to those *things*. Plus, she got goose bumps as she got nearer until her skin felt like it was crawling with ants. That didn't seem like any hallucinations she had read about on the internet.

The first time it had happened was barely twenty-four hours after she had activated the Golem. Naomi had been at one of the mandatory pre–Bat Mitzvah Friday-night services when she started hearing whispering around her. She thought that maybe some of the grandmas in the back of the sanctuary were gossiping through the sermon again, but when she looked around, everyone was sitting quietly, watching Rabbi Levinson as he talked. The whispering had gotten louder, though, and Naomi was still looking for

something else entirely. Then Eitan, still a little pale, pulled out his journal and sat right down in the wood chips with her, saying simply, "Tell me every detail again. We need to make sure we're keeping track." Becca had sat down too, though she let go of Naomi's sweaty hands with a small wrinkle in her nose, and that was that.

It didn't stop there, though. That same evening, after services, a girl in an old-fashioned dress had followed Naomi and her mama around the grocery store, watching Naomi intently with too-dark eyes. Naomi had felt that stare on the back of her neck no matter where she went in the store and could do nothing but try to ignore the itchiness of goose bumps that had nothing to do with the chill of the freezer aisle. She was trying to ignore the things, mostly, but she couldn't help the sharp bite of fear and adrenaline that rushed through her every time she realized there was something decidedly *not human* watching her. She had tried to point out other, smaller sightings of the weird, non-human people to Becca and Eitan while they were out during the day, but they never saw any of it. Just like they couldn't see or hear the other muttering, shadowy ghosts that had popped up in the corners of the synagogue after they went back inside, and like they were never able to make the Golem do things.

Now there was a man smiling at Naomi from the other side of the bus stop bench in front of the arcade, and Naomi was alone with nothing but her phone to pretend to focus on. Eitan had tried to wait with her for as long as he could, but they had played long enough that he was late for chess club and had to race there on his bike. It was fine. Naomi didn't need someone to wait for the bus with her. Still, she wished she had brought her headphones. Music did nothing to drown out the whispers in her mind that warned her something not entirely human was nearby, but her skin was crawling with goose bumps under her sweater, and she desperately wanted a distraction. If nothing else, headphones would have helped her look busy, at least. She darted a nervous glance sideways. The man was still smiling intently at her.

It wasn't totally out of the ordinary for weird, gross men to stare at her; Naomi was almost thirteen, and sometimes people were creepy at the bus stop. But this man was different. He was wrapped up from his neck to his shoes in black, too warm for the Southern California winter, and he was wearing dark glasses that reflected everything around him, so Naomi couldn't see his eyes. Every time she snuck a look his way, he smiled with teeth that seemed just a bit too big and sharp to be normal. When she accidentally caught his eye—well, his glasses—a strange hissing joined the whispers in the back of her mind that felt very, very wrong. Like a spider-sense screaming *Danger!*

Naomi tapped her fingers uselessly against her phone screen, pins and needles pricking their way from her fingertips up her arms. She swallowed the panic that was crawling up her throat, threatening to choke her. Eitan hadn't seen the man in black at the bus stop before he left, and Naomi hadn't wanted to tell him about it in case he decided to stay with her. She didn't want him to get in trouble for missing chess club when they wouldn't have a good explanation for it. She was regretting that a little now. The creepy man sidled closer along the bench, and Naomi tried to inch behind the dad with the baby on her other side. The baby waved at her, and Naomi mustered up a tense smile, still scooting sideways to put the dad between her and the man in black. The man showed his teeth again. Naomi willed the bus to come faster.

The bus came, and Naomi almost cried in relief when the sharp-toothed man stayed at the bus stop. He wiggled his fingers at her as the bus drove away, but Naomi turned her head and stared forward out the front window all the way home, refusing to make eye contact with anyone. She made it up the stairs to her room and flopped down on her bed with a pillow hugged tightly to her chest until she felt like she could breathe again, the pins-and-needles feeling retreating to the usual faint buzzing under her skin that was present whenever the Golem was nearby. The bedspread smelled like fresh dryer sheets, and Naomi rubbed her nose against it, inhaling the clean, soft scent and trying to convince her heart to slow down.

"Golem," she whispered. A small weight joined her on the bed, and Naomi turned her head enough to blink owlishly at the Golem. "Is this your fault?" she asked. It stared back at her, quiet as ever. Naomi sighed. "Figures. All right, fine, no answers. Then will you at least get me

some gummy worms? I've earned comfort food."
The Golem disappeared off the bed and trotted
out the door.

Naomi stared after it. She couldn't be totally
sure, but it didn't seem to be *quite* as little as it
had been when she'd woken it up. It was definitely moving better, almost as smoothly as a
real person. In fact, the Golem was so lifelike now
that Naomi was starting to feel bad about calling
it "it," though she wasn't sure what else to call it.
Her parents were very specific on their feelings
about giving other things genders without asking, and Naomi had taken those lessons to heart,
but she really wanted to just call the little clay
figure "he." It was probably fine, she decided. It
was like a stuffed toy or a car. Nobody got mad
when Naomi decided her stuffed giraffe Wally
was a boy or when her uncle Len called his car a
lady—though Naomi personally thought that one
was a little weird. Anyway, *he* was certainly better
than *it*, even if gender didn't really apply. Naomi
had made an attempt just that morning to ask the
Golem if it had a gender, or if it wanted one, and
had been met with the same placid indifference
she received whenever she said anything to the

Golem that wasn't a direct request. She figured that meant it didn't mind.

The Golem ducked back around her slightly open door and tripped along the strip of carpet Naomi had cleared of her typical mess so it— no, *he*—could go back and forth more easily. He was carrying a pack of sour gummy worms high above his head. He was definitely growing, Naomi decided. The day before, he had gotten her some pretzels and had to drag the bag behind him on the floor, and she was pretty sure that the gummy worms had to be heavier than the pretzels. She wondered if that was supposed to happen. Was the growing just a phase, like some sort of Golem puberty? Mostly, Naomi wanted to know if there was a point where he would *stop*.

It had been pretty easy to keep him hidden from her moms and Deena so far. Even after his very small growth spurt, the Golem was tiny, and Naomi's moms were working for most of the day. Deena was always home, but she rarely came out of her room. Mama said Deena was "going through it," which meant absolutely nothing to Naomi but made any other adults around nod understandingly. Still, even with Deena's mysterious ordeals keeping her from paying too much attention to Naomi, the Golem was going to be harder to hide if he got too big to keep in her bedside table. Naomi wasn't sure what she was going to do then.

More worryingly, it had been only two days, and already Naomi's strange encounters with the people-shaped *things* only she could see seemed to be escalating. The man at the bus stop had felt much scarier than the little girl at the store; the warnings in Naomi's head had seemed much louder, and the prickling of weird magic across her skin had been almost unbearable. There was a terrible theory floating around in the back of Naomi's mind that the bigger the Golem got, the more dangerous the creatures she met would be. She was certain that if she wasn't hallucinating (and she had decided that she wasn't), then the two things were linked. It wasn't like she had been having supernatural encounters *before*, and the timing was too spot-on for there to be any other explanation.

Naomi prodded at the gummy worm package and then prodded at the Golem, looking at the trail of faint glowing footprints he had left behind as he walked. Those were also a concern, as they weren't exactly *subtle*. Eitan and Becca couldn't see those, either, though, so it was possible that was *another* thing specific to Naomi. It made her feel a bit crazy. It also made her afraid to ask the Golem for too much, in case people did start to notice the weird occurrences around him. So far Naomi had kept the requests she made of the Golem small and within a few rooms of whatever space she was in, but Eitan was pushing for Naomi to try bigger tests, insisting they needed more information, and Becca seemed to agree. Naomi couldn't help but think that was easy for them to say. She took the gummy worms from the Golem and patted his head absentmindedly.

"Thanks, little buddy." The Golem stood for a moment, processing that this meant his task was complete, then hoisted himself up onto the bed using the dangling edge of Naomi's comforter. Naomi watched him as he settled in next to her, becoming still and lifeless again as he waited for her next request. He seemed content. Naomi gnawed on her thumbnail and thought, *That makes one of us.*

She tried to watch TV on her computer for a while, angling the screen so the Golem could see, just in case he was interested. She queued up her favorite cartoon, something bright and silly that always made her feel better, but she couldn't focus. She felt restless and unsettled, like she had forgotten to do a big homework assignment but couldn't remember what it was. Finally, she had to admit that she couldn't remember anything about the three episodes she had just watched. Her mind was too full of questions. All she wanted were some answers before things got out of hand, but maybe Eitan and Becca were right, and she wasn't going to learn anything if she kept doing the same things over and over.

"Okay," Naomi decided suddenly, "we're going to try something new." She pulled out her phone and set up a three-way video call with Eitan and Becca. "Okay," Naomi said again, once they were both on-screen, "who's somewhere I can send a Golem?"

Eitan scoffed. "You're kidding me, Nae. You want to send it out of the house? Yesterday you literally said 'never.'"

"That was yesterday," Naomi said dismissively. "I want to try this. I think he can do it."

"Oh, we're calling it a *he* now?" Becca asked.

She squinted at the phone, like she was trying to see the Golem better. "Did it develop genitalia?"

Naomi fought the urge to cover the Golem's ears. "Shut up," she said, though Becca was probably genuinely asking; she rarely asked questions she didn't actually want to know the answer to. "He's been really reliable around the house. I want to see if he can run errands between us. He's probably too conspicuous to take to school, but he's getting faster. Imagine if we could use him to pick up snacks? Or send stuff back and forth even when we're grounded and can't use our phones?"

She tried to make her voice sound excited, instead of full of the shaky doubt she was feeling. It was true, anyway. Things might have been getting a little weird, but there was no reason they couldn't use the Golem in the meantime. He *wanted* to help them!

Her words were met with the thoughtful silence of people who hadn't yet considered the possibilities of having a tiny, sneaky ally.

"You're not wrong," Eitan said slowly. "All right, well, I'm home from chess club, and no one else will be around until five. I could do it."

Becca groaned loudly. "I wanted to take him!"

"All right," Eitan said easily. "I'm not stressed about it. You can have the trial run."

"No." Becca sighed. "I'm at the dentist." She flashed her phone around to show them the drab, slightly run-down front of their local pediatric dentist's office. Eitan and Naomi groaned in empathy. They all went to the same dentist. Dr. Hill used gross bubble-gum-flavored toothpaste and always smelled like tuna fish. "I came outside to talk," Becca said, "but I'm pretty sure my mom's going to make me go first so Ariela and Benji don't get scared again. Last time Benji cried so hard they had to give him laughing gas just to chill him out enough to open his mouth."

"Yeesh," Naomi said. "What about Jake? Does he not get scared?"

Becca sighed again. It was a familiar sigh of deep disappointment with the second-oldest Reznik sibling. Jake Reznik was eleven years old, and a menace. "*No*," Becca said. "Jake's not allowed back until he promises to stop biting the dentist." Eitan gave a loud snort, which he tried unsuccessfully to cover up with a cough. Becca glared. "It's not funny. Jake almost got us all banned!"

"Banned from the dentist isn't so bad," Naomi said, "but that's not really the point. Sorry, Becks. You'll have to be trial two."

"That's fine. You all just have fun playing with the magical helper toy, and I'll be here, getting my mouth-bones scraped."

Eitan said, "Ew," which pretty much summed it up, in Naomi's opinion.

"Great. Best of luck with that. We'll update you when you're done!" She hung up Becca's portion of the call and focused on Eitan. "What do you want him to bring you?"

Eitan squinted at her. "What are you eating?"

"Sour gummy worms."

"I want those."

Naomi clutched the bag to her chest protectively. "No way, bud. These are *my* hard-earned contraband."

"Come on, Nae," Eitan whined. "Share the spoils."

"Not happening." Naomi thought about things she could send over to Eitan that would be easy for the Golem to carry. "I'll send you a Three Musketeers." That was a fair offer, she thought. A chocolate bar was a reasonable thing to ask the

Golem to carry the few miles to Eitan's house, and Eitan loved Three Musketeers, even though Naomi personally didn't see the appeal. She tended to hoard them whenever she got them, though, to be used as bribes when she needed something from Eitan, whose parents were very strict about their only son's sugar intake.

Eitan, it seemed, agreed. "Deal," he said. "Send him over. It's good timing anyway. I've been doing some research, and it would be cool to get another close look at him."

Naomi nodded absently. Eitan knew the most about Golems from all the stories he had read when they were younger, and he was constantly doing research, though Naomi couldn't figure out where he was getting his information. She definitely hadn't been able to find anything on the internet in the searches she had done to try to find out more about Golems. Maybe Eitan was just better at internet searches than her. He was absolutely more excited about research than she was. Naomi figured it was easier just to let him tell her what he found. She fished the candy bar out of the secret stash in her nightstand and handed it to the Golem. "Okay, buddy," she said. "You're going to take this to Eitan." After a moment's thought, she told the Golem Eitan's address as well, just to be sure. "Anything else you can think of?" she asked her friend, who was watching the process with his notebook clutched in one hand and his face pressed close to the camera of his phone.

Eitan tapped his pen against his chin and hummed, making the speaker go staticky for a moment. "Did you remember to tell it to come back?"

"*Him*," Naomi corrected. "But you're right." She turned to the Golem. "When you're done, I want you to come right back to me. No, wait!" She thought quickly, watching as the little figure began to stir. "I want you to stay with Eitan and do what he asks until he tells you to come back."

"You don't think that's a little complicated?" Eitan's face on her phone screen was skeptical.

Naomi shrugged, a little reckless. Now that she had taken this first big step, she wanted to push. "Won't know till we try it."

"What if he gets lost?"

"I can find him," Naomi said confidently.

"By his glowing lava footprints?"

"They're real!"

Eitan held up his hand, waving his notebook around like he was trying to fan away Naomi's glare. "Okay, fine, sorry! I believe that you can see his sparkly footprints, jeez. Send him over! I'll be here, waiting for the terrifying candy gram."

"Cool," Naomi said. She turned back to the Golem. "Take the chocolate to Eitan, and stay with him until he tells you to come back. While you're with him, you help him, okay?"

The Golem didn't nod. The Golem never nodded. Regardless, Naomi was sure that he understood. He always understood her orders. He slid back down her comforter, hefted the chocolate onto his shoulder, and marched out the door.

"He's on his way," Naomi told Eitan.

"All right, I'll call you when he's here."

It didn't occur to Naomi until the Golem had already been gone for half an hour that three miles was an awfully long way to go on tiny clay legs. The Golem didn't move that quickly. It took him five minutes just to get to the kitchen and back. Naomi groaned and flopped back onto her bed, dropping the book she was reading on her face. At that pace, it would take the Golem hours to reach Eitan. The Golem was probably sneaky enough to get by Eitan's parents, but even so, Naomi couldn't help but feel that they were cutting it close. She really should have thought it through better.

Naomi fretted for another fifteen minutes, trying to read and unable to stop worrying, before deciding that she was just going to get on her bike and go after him. She could find him by his footprints, whatever Eitan believed. She would bring him home, and they would try again tomorrow when Becca was home. Her house was much closer to Naomi's. That would be a better start. She snuck downstairs as quietly as she could—the last thing she needed was Deena coming out of her room and asking questions—and was just pulling her jacket out of the hall closet when her phone rang. It was Eitan. Naomi frowned. It hadn't even been an hour.

"Hello?"

Eitan's face appeared on the screen, his mouth full of chocolate. "He's here," he said, "and the chocolate's intact, but, Nae, I think we might have a bit of a problem." He held the phone out so Naomi could see the Golem sitting on Eitan's beanbag chair. Naomi's brain was so full of racing thoughts about how the Golem could have possibly gotten three miles in less than an hour on its tiny little legs, she almost didn't realize what she was looking at until Eitan said it:

"He's bigger."

4

THE SITUATION GETS
A LITTLE BIGGER

The Golem was now the size of one of Naomi's old American Girl dolls. This was good, because it meant Naomi could give it a small backpack to hold things in and a fluffy little coat to wear, which was cute. It was also decidedly *not good*, since Naomi now had a clay man the size of a large doll following her around. There was no way her family wouldn't notice eventually.

"Why does he keep getting bigger?" Naomi demanded. Becca, lying on her back across her bed, threw her softball above her head and caught it a couple of times before she answered.

"No idea."

Naomi reached out and tried to snag the ball out of the air before Becca could catch it, but her reflexes weren't quick enough. She was in the theater club, which didn't require a whole lot of hand-eye coordination beyond making it to her mark on time. Becca didn't even fumble the ball, just caught it and rolled over to smirk at Naomi. Naomi made a gesture that would have gotten her in trouble if either of her moms had seen it.

Becca rolled her eyes. "I don't know why you're mad at *me*! You're the one in charge of the fantastic growing Golem. Maybe you could try telling him to be small again."

"I *have* tried that." Naomi huffed. "It didn't work. Anyway, I don't know what's making him grow."

"I do."

Both girls looked up as Eitan shouldered his way into the room, his backpack nearly bursting with his sleepover gear and whatever board games and snacks he had brought with him. They were backyard camping at Becca's house. Naomi had packed almost nothing, since she needed to take the Golem with her, and she didn't have a good explanation for having two bags when her mama dropped her off. She could probably have told the Golem to just meet her there, but she wasn't willing to risk another giant growth spurt, so into the backpack he went. It was fine. Naomi wore Becca's clothes all the time. Becca was broader in the shoulders, but Naomi was taller, so they ended up wearing about the same size. Besides, Naomi would rather have Becca's hand-me-overs than Deena's hand-me-downs any day; Becca's clothes were always super soft. Eitan dropped his bag onto the floor of Becca's room and joined them on the bed, flopping onto his stomach next to Becca. The Golem was sitting quietly on Becca's desk chair, waiting for a job. Eitan burst out laughing when he saw him.

"Love the makeover," he told Naomi. "Teal is definitely his color."

"Look, if he's going to be the size of an American Girl, he's going to wear the clothes. It's the only good thing I have left in this madness."

Becca scoffed. "Don't be so dramatic. Maybe he's done growing."

"He's not," Eitan said. "I told you, I know what's making him get bigger." He lifted his head and cast a superior look at the two of them. "And *you* only don't know because you haven't read any of the notes I sent you." Naomi and Becca groaned in unison.

"Why would we read the notes you send us when you're going to tell us anyway?" Becca asked.

Eitan glared. "One day I'm going to stop telling you things and just watch you crash and burn."

Becca met him glare for glare. "You wouldn't."

Eitan blinked first. He sighed. "No, probably not."

"*Guys*," Naomi said, "can we get back to this actual real problem I'm dealing with?"

"Sorry, Nae." Eitan rolled over so he could sit up and dragged his bag toward him, rummaging around in the front pouch. "Okay, watch. Naomi, have him come here."

"Golem, come over here," Naomi called. The Golem raised his head at the sound of her voice, then clambered down from the desk chair and walked over to stand at attention in front of Naomi. "Good job," Naomi said absently, then to Eitan, "Now what?"

Eitan grunted and continued his search for a moment. Then he pulled out a tape measure from his backpack triumphantly. He stuck the little metal bit under the Golem's foot, then stretched the tape out until it reached the top of the Golem's head. "Forty-six centimeters," he announced. "Wow, he really is the same height as those American Girl dolls."

There was a pause.

"Why do you know the exact height of an American Girl doll off the top of your head?" Becca asked.

"I don't question *your* strange knowledge about maps, Becks," Eitan said loftily.

"He made a cake for his cousin's birthday party last year and she wanted an American Girl one," Naomi said.

Eitan glared. "Wow. Betrayal. Ruining my mystique. And I'm being so helpful."

"Are you?" Naomi asked.

"Yes." He took the tape measure away and nodded at her. "Okay, now tell him to do something."

Naomi blinked. "Um. Okay? Golem, will you set up the tent for us in the backyard?"

"Wow, lazy much?" Becca said, but the Golem was already moving. Fast. He was out of the room and poking around the pile of orange nylon and metal poles before the three of them realized he had gone. They scrambled to the window, shoving at one another and pressing their faces against the glass to see what the Golem was doing. Much faster than they would have been able to— and definitely faster than *he* would have been able to just the day before—the little clay man drove stakes into the ground, threaded the poles through the tent fabric, and raised the tent and its tarp in the span of about five minutes. Then he was gone from the yard. There was a soft thump on the rug behind them. Naomi felt her heart in her throat as the three of them turned away from the window to see the Golem standing patiently in the middle of Becca's room once more. It might have been Naomi's imagination that the sleeves of the fluffy teal jacket she had dressed him in were sitting a little farther up his arms, but she didn't think it was.

Moving slowly, as though he were afraid that *now* the Golem might spook, Eitan retrieved the tape measure and repeated the process of measuring the Golem. "Forty-nine centimeters," he announced.

"Seriously?" Naomi demanded. Next to her, Becca was looking a bit like she was about to have a heart attack, which seemed unfair. *Naomi* was the one who was going to have to hide the thing from her moms when he was the size of a large dog. "He gets bigger when he does things I ask him to?"

Eitan nodded. "The bigger the task, the bigger the growth spurt," he said. "That's why when he was just getting candy in from the kitchen you didn't notice it as much, but he shot up when you sent him to me."

Becca said faintly, "Holy smokes."

"That feels like something they should have put on the label," Naomi said. She was beginning to feel that same sense of unease she had when she first activated the Golem. The same flutter of *wrongness* that accompanied each strange encounter she'd had with those terrifying new creature-people out in the world. It was worse now, grown bigger with the Golem like she'd worried it would. She felt panic gathering underneath her rib cage like there were important things she was missing, and the situation was rapidly spiraling out of her control.

"They didn't put *anything* on the label," Becca reminded her.

"Well, that was the first red flag," Eitan said. "Shoddy instruction manuals are never a good sign."

Naomi rounded on him. "Could you take this seriously for, like, one second? I know *you* think it's fun and cool, but *I've* got creepy, not-really-people things following me at the grocery store and stalking me at the bus stop. I'm hearing, like, magical warning whispers in my head all the time, and I am seeing literal *ghosts* every time I go to temple! Plus, if my moms find out I've got this weird magic helper thing, they're going to lose it. Mama is going to try to cleanse the whole house, and you know Mom will, like, call Homeland Security or the governor or Area 51!" She stomped her foot, feeling a little childish but unable to help it. "They'll think someone sent me something dangerous, and then the government will take him away and do experiments on him or something. He's *my* responsibility! We need to figure this out!"

Her friends were quiet. Eitan, at least, looked awkwardly sorry. It could be hard to tell with

Becca, who didn't always do facial expressions the same way Naomi and Eitan did, but the twist to the corner of her mouth told Naomi that Becca was probably feeling uncomfortable. Then Eitan said hesitantly, "*Did* someone send you something dangerous?" The three of them looked at the Golem, standing serenely on the light-blue carpet of Becca's bedroom. If he noticed the scrutiny, he didn't react. Becca was fidgeting with her softball. Eitan had shifted closer to Naomi, though she wasn't sure if he realized. "You said you've been seeing . . . other things. Is he doing something to you?"

"*He's* not dangerous," Naomi said, wishing she sounded more sure. "I really don't know about everything else, but *he's* here to help. Right?"

Eitan asked, "To help who?" It wasn't the kind of question Naomi wanted to hear from her friends, even if it was one she had been wondering herself.

"Well," Becca said, "it is Naomi's name on the scroll, right? That means he's here to help *her*, doesn't it?"

"Right!" said Naomi. "Someone sent him to me. It's my name on the scroll. I'm in charge. He's not dangerous."

"If only we could ask him." Eitan sighed. "All right, fine. Arguing about this isn't helping. You already asked your moms who sent it, and they don't know. There's no record of him coming through the mail, and no one's been checking in about him. I trust you to know what you're doing, Nae, but even if he's not meant to be dangerous, we have bigger problems on our hands. Literally." Eitan gestured at the Golem with the measuring tape, looking like he agreed wholeheartedly with Becca's earlier assessment of "holy smokes." "One, I've been reading more about Jewish magic in general, and I'm pretty sure that the not-really-people things Naomi is seeing are demons."

"What?" The girls were so loud that Eitan took a step backward.

"I'm just saying, demons in Jewish folklore seem like they kind of look and act like whatever they want, and all of them want to trap people in the demon world or dimension or whatever they call it. It sounds right, doesn't it?"

Naomi shuddered. "I wish it didn't."

Becca patted Naomi's shoulder as Eitan said grimly, "Well, whatever they are, what happens when one of them decides to do more than follow

Naomi?" They all winced. "And two," Eitan went on, "someone is bound to notice him if he keeps growing, no matter how helpful he is."

"Okay, so how do we stop him from growing more?" Becca asked. "Naomi already tried telling him to be smaller."

Eitan looked thoughtful. "What if you just stopped using him?"

"Stopped using him?" Naomi echoed.

"Sure." Eitan shrugged. "If he gets bigger every time you ask him to do something, then it makes sense that if you stopped asking him to do things, he would stop growing."

"It does," Naomi said slowly, "but it seems like kind of a waste, right? Like if someone gave you a magic wand and then you just put it in a case."

Becca snorted. "He's not a magic wand. He's a glorified grabber claw. You can survive fetching your own snacks again, Nae."

Naomi felt her face flush. "It's not about that! He just . . ." She trailed off. The Golem continued to stand rigid and still in the middle of the room, his blank face somehow expectant. "He seems happier when he has things to do."

Eitan hummed thoughtfully, but Becca just

scoffed again. "He's a statue, Nae. He's clay that someone figured out how to animate. He's not feeling anything. Stop telling him to do things, and he won't grow. Simple, right?" She nodded, like she was answering her own question. With some effort, she picked up the Golem and sat him on her bed with her stuffed toys, arranging her teddy bears around him like he could blend in if she tried hard enough. "There," she said. "He can stay there for now. The siblings know they're not allowed to touch anything on my bed." She gave Naomi a little shove and reached behind her to grab hold of Eitan's shirt and pull him along. "C'mon. Let's go *camping*."

Things were not, it turned out, as simple as Becca had made them seem. For one thing, Naomi didn't actually have anywhere to store the Golem that didn't leave her feeling guilty. When he was tiny, she had kept him in her bedside table, and after that she had hidden him under her bed, but that had been when she was pulling him out every few hours to give him a task. Without that, it just felt like she was shutting him up in the dark. Finally, Naomi compromised by putting the Golem in the large toy chest at the foot of her bed. It was still dark, but she hoped he wouldn't be as lonely with all the other dolls and board games in there.

It was silly, she knew. Becca laughed at her when Naomi told her and Eitan about her dilemma, but Naomi knew for a fact that Becca kept her maps of the county and the greater L.A. area sorted in a specific color gradient because she believed the colors affected the maps' "moods," so she didn't have a lot of room to talk. Eitan didn't laugh; he just raised his eyebrows thoughtfully, like this was another piece of Golem information for him to stow away.

The next couple of days after that were a blur. Naomi tried hard. It was difficult to ignore the strangeness that was popping up around her with increasing frequency. The morning after their camping night, an old lady approached Naomi at the mini golf course when Becca and Eitan went to buy snacks. The woman grabbed Naomi's wrist in an iron-strong grip and offered her a handful of candy. When Naomi said no, the woman twisted her wrinkled face into an expression that might have been close to a smile and offered to tell Naomi's fortune, her raspy voice making a strange chorus with the whispering voices in Naomi's head. Sharp nails had grown like talons to dig into her wrist as her skin tingled with warning and magic. Naomi wasn't sure how long she had been held in the old woman's dark gaze before a family came over the hill by the windmill and startled Naomi back into herself. The woman had disappeared so quickly, Naomi wasn't sure she hadn't actually vanished. The scratches on Naomi's arm had stayed, red and itchy.

At home, things were worse in a different way. The Golem lasted a day in the toy chest, keeping as still and silent as he always was when he was waiting for a task, quiet in the trunk at the foot of her bed like he had never moved at all. It made Naomi hope, for a short, wonderful moment, that maybe Becca had been right and that really would be the end of it. It wasn't.

On the second day, Naomi woke up early to a strange sense of restless energy in her room. Her bed was shaking, she realized. Small, almost unnoticeable vibrations were running from the foot of the bed up to the headboard. Something was moving in the toy chest. Naomi crawled to the foot of her bed and leaned over to peer at the chest. She placed a nervous hand on the lid. Sure enough, it was shaking slightly, like something inside it was rocking back and forth very quickly. Naomi threw open the lid, her heart in her throat, and was both immensely relieved and not at all surprised to see the Golem go still, his expectant gaze trained on her face.

"Stop that," she told him. "There's no reason to be dramatic about this."

The Golem, predictably, said nothing. Though Naomi felt that there was something scornful in his featureless face. She sighed. "If you can't stop growing when you do things, you can't do things—it's as simple as that." She parroted Becca's words from the weekend, though even to her own ears they sounded unconvincing. The Golem stayed blank and still, and Naomi sighed again. "It's too early for this. Can you chill out for a few hours at least?" She waited a moment, then shut the lid of the toy chest and sat back on her bed. The shaking didn't start up again, so she figured the Golem had taken "chill out" as a task. She pulled her blankets over her head and went back to sleep.

On the third day, Naomi had to take the Golem

out of the trunk or risk the whole thing shaking apart into little pieces. Once free, the Golem paced in tiny circles on her carpet, his little limbs swinging in sharp, jerky motions and his rough features trained on Naomi as much as they could be while moving in circles that quickly. It was almost like watching a dancer spot their turns but much more disconcerting. Telling him to chill out only made him stutter to a graceless halt for a moment or two and then start up again. Inaction, apparently, could only work as a task for so long. Naomi sat on the floor and watched the Golem move in his frantic little circles for a few long, helpless minutes. Then she took a video and sent it to the group chat.

Any suggestions?

There was a lull while they caught up, and then there was a long stretch of time while one or both of her friends typed and deleted whatever they were thinking. Finally, just when Naomi was beginning to get really impatient, Eitan responded, **WHAT?**

Naomi rolled her eyes. **Helpful.**

Literally, though, what??? That was Becca.

He's been like this all morning, Naomi told them.

I don't think he's doing well with the whole No Tasks thing. She waited a minute and then sent, **Telling him to chill out stopped working pretty quickly.**

Naomi's phone rang a second later. Eitan. "Holy heck, Nae," he breathed when she held the phone up so he could watch the Golem in real time.

"Tell me about it."

"Okay," he said, "okay." Then again, "Okay." Before he could really start to freak out, Naomi's phone beeped with an alert that Becca was trying to call in.

"I'm conferencing Becca in," she warned.

Becca's "holy smokes" was just as unhelpful as Eitan's "okay"s.

"I'm going to give him things to do," Naomi said, raising her voice to talk over her friends' excited babbling. It was rude, but if they weren't going to be helpful, they at least could have tried not to make her more anxious. "He needs to do something! I'll keep it little. Maybe if he never leaves the room, he won't— GUYS!" she shouted. Her friends quieted, and Naomi took a breath. "As I was saying. Maybe if he never leaves the room, he won't be able to grow very much." She sat down on her bed. "Here, let's try this. Golem, will you get me a pencil?"

The Golem *blurred*. Naomi wasn't sure where he went, but he returned a few minutes later with a brand-new, bright green, sparkly mechanical pencil that Naomi had never seen before in her life. It was the same brand all the kids at school were clamoring to get ahold of—they had been sold out at every office supply store Naomi had dragged her mama to over fall break, and she hadn't been able to convince either of her moms to try to look for them again since then. The Golem presented the pencil to her with the kind of satisfaction Naomi had only ever seen in Becca's cat after it caught a bird. He was visibly taller.

Naomi held up the phone, and Becca said a word that they were definitely not supposed to know. "Yeah," Naomi breathed. "I'm with you." She took the pencil and patted the Golem's head gingerly in thanks. He settled into quiet stillness again, like he hadn't just been wearing a hole in Naomi's carpet with his jittery pacing. Naomi bit her lip. "Okay, let's try this again. Golem, will you bring me the yellow pencil that is sitting on my desk?"

The Golem walked calmly across the room, as if to prove he could, and retrieved the pencil for her. If he grew, Naomi couldn't tell.

"Okay, so you just have to be super specific," Eitan said. "Super, *super* specific. Nae, you can work with that, right?"

Naomi looked at the Golem, that unnamed worry building in her stomach again.

"Right," she said.

Naomi tried, she really did, but the Golem didn't do well with tiny tasks. He got more and more restless by the hour, until Naomi had to give him more to do or risk getting caught because of the noise. She tried to keep the tasks small and focused, but even with her best efforts, the Golem was getting bigger. Less than a day later, he was up to her waist. There wasn't even space in her closet for her to keep him without shoving him on top of a pile of shoes. Naomi finally started to just lock her room when she left, rather than trying to hide the Golem anywhere. She had also taken to throwing bits of paper across the carpet and asking him to bring them back to her just to get rid of some of the Golem's restless energy, though she could tell, somehow, that that wouldn't last long either. A Golem needed a purpose.

It wasn't just the Golem. Things outside were getting worse, too. Naomi couldn't ride the bus alone anymore. The man in black was always there at the bus stop, leering at her with his shiny sunglasses and his too-sharp teeth. If Naomi was alone, he would slowly inch closer without seeming to move a muscle. So far, the bus had come before the man had reached her, but Naomi didn't want to find out what would happen if he did. It didn't matter where she went; strange people with inviting smiles and limbs that didn't seem to move quite right offered her fancy cell phones and unlimited credit cards if she just helped them with their flat tire, their lost dog, or their stuck kite.

Naomi felt bad sometimes. She worried that maybe there really were people who needed her help, but the buzzing whisper in her head that warned of danger always screamed at her when she hesitated for too long, and the people's eyes grew hungry and dangerous. It was barely safe to ride her bike. The whispers in her head never stopped, and Naomi was always afraid of stopping in one place for too long. She started sticking around home, venturing out only when one of her moms or Deena could drive her places. Naomi felt like she was going crazy, and through it all, the Golem continued to grow.

It all came to a head when Naomi was with her family. It was pizza night, and Mom was bickering with Deena about getting off her phone, while Mama pulled out ingredients for the dough and told Naomi a story about one of her yoga students.

"And then—I swear, Nomes, I can't make this stuff up—she said, 'No, it's okay. I'm comfortable like this!'" Mama dissolved into laughter, and Naomi smiled, laughing more at how tickled her mama was than at the unfortunate yoga student getting stuck in their pose. Then her smile froze on her face. Her mama made a concerned noise. "Nomes? You okay, sweetie?"

Naomi dragged her eyes away from the shadowy figure of the Golem on the stairs and nodded vigorously. "Yeah, Mama. Definitely. I just remembered"—she remembered just in time that it was winter break and cast about wildly for an excuse that wasn't homework—"I remembered that I told Eitan I'd help him bake a cake for Cantor Debbie.

You know, as a thank-you for helping us with our Torah portions."

Mama's eyes widened. "Oh, that's a lovely idea, Nomes. That's so sweet of you, but—"

The Golem on the stairs was blurring slightly, like he was shivering. Naomi could feel the whispery voices that echoed in her head when she was near something inhuman grow loud and insistent, though she had never heard them because of the Golem before. The Golem had never come to find her on his own before, either. Something was wrong. Naomi shook her head sharply at whatever her mama was saying. "Sorry, Mama! I'm just really, really late. Eitan is just blowing up my phone, you know?" She waved her dark, notification-less phone at her mama and pushed herself back from the table. "I'll be home by the time the pizza's ready! Swear it!" She kissed her bewildered mama's cheek and rushed toward the stairs, calling out, "Bye, Mom! Bye Deens!" as she went.

She caught the twitching Golem by the hand and barreled up the stairs with him, ignoring her mom's call of, "Naomi, that's the wrong way to the front door!"

She got back into her room and knelt in front of the Golem, her chest tight with fear and frustration. He seemed calmer now that she was focusing on him, which made her weirdly angry. "You can't *do* that!" she said. "What if they had seen you?" Naomi drummed her fingers on her knees, staring at the Golem but not really seeing him, trying to think. "Okay," she told him. "We're going to the park. Go out the window and meet me there. Don't let my family see you!" Naomi didn't wait to see if he went—she'd had the Golem long enough to know that, strange behavior or not, if she told him to do something, it would get done. She trundled back down the stairs, waving her jacket at her Mom in explanation for going to her room first, and then sprinted for her bike. She tossed her phone in the basket, yelling for it to call Eitan.

"Call Becca," she said as soon as he answered. "We're meeting at the park in ten minutes. This isn't working."

5

NAOMI PUTS
HER FOOT DOWN

The park was deserted when Naomi got there, the sun just beginning to disappear below the horizon. She parked her bike at the rack and sat on the swings to wait. It didn't take long. Naomi had barely started to move her legs when the Golem appeared beside her, looking almost threatening in the half-light. The whispering voices—gentler, somehow, than when they warned Naomi against the things Eitan kept insisting were definitely demons of some kind—appeared with it. Naomi hissed in surprise and pushed off the swing, but then the Golem followed her as she moved into the glow of a streetlamp, and he was the same strange little creature she had been dealing with for more than a week. She patted his head like she always did when he completed a task, but this time he didn't go still the way he usually did. He watched her silently, calm but obviously waiting. He looked like he had gained another inch or two during his journey. Naomi gritted her teeth.

She turned her gaze away from him and back to the wide expanse of the park. The Golem's glowing footsteps crisscrossing the darkened grass burned in Naomi's vision. "We're waiting for Eitan and Becca," she told him, more to fill the silence than because she thought he cared. He was a very single-minded being. "They'll be here in a minute."

It was actually seven minutes, but Becca finally rolled in on her skateboard, Eitan on his bike close behind.

"He's bigger!" Becca said accusingly as soon as she got to the swings. "I thought you were being careful, Nae!"

Naomi glared at her, though she was sure the effect was lost in the dark. "I was! I am!" She groaned. "I don't know how to stop him from doing it."

"So what, we're here to figure out a new place to hide him?" Eitan asked, coming up behind Becca and propping his elbow on her shoulder. She jabbed at his side and he stepped back, hands up. "Easy there, Becks. No need to get violent."

Becca hissed.

"*Guys*," Naomi said sharply, "*please*." They both looked up, all play-fighting forgotten at her tone.

"Are you okay, Nae?" Eitan asked hesitantly.

"No!" Naomi cried. She felt tears gathering in the corners of her eyes and scrubbed at them angrily. "I don't know what to *do*! He's too big, and he won't stay hidden, and soon someone is going to see him and take him away! And every time he grows, the other weird things get worse, and other people are starting to notice! You guys saw that old lady at the mini golf place, and yesterday Deena swore she saw something following us at the mall that didn't look *human*." She stopped, breathing hard and unable to keep the tears from spilling down her cheeks. "I don't know what to do," she said again.

Wordlessly, Becca stepped closer until Naomi could pitch forward and rest her face against her shoulder. It was a familiar motion. Becca didn't really hug, but she knew that Naomi sometimes needed it, so she would often scoot just close enough that Naomi could lean on her without actually hugging. Then Eitan, as he often did, ruined the whole carefully balanced routine by stepping up and wrapping his arms firmly around both of them. Becca let out an exasperated sigh through her nose but didn't protest or try to elbow him again.

"We're going to figure it out, Nae," Eitan said. "We're the dream team; we've got this."

Naomi sniffed, then prodded at her friends until Becca could step back with a grateful huff of air and Naomi could turn fully to hug Eitan, who was more than happy to oblige. "How?" she asked.

"Can you just . . . set him free?" Becca asked.

"Without knowing who sent him to her?" Eitan asked. He was chewing on his thumbnail hard enough that there was blood welling up along his cuticles. He hadn't done that since his mom had broken him of the habit by dipping his thumbs in spicy mustard for two weeks when they were in the fifth grade. Naomi automatically reached out and pulled his hand down. He grabbed her hand and squeezed. "I don't want to make it worse, Nae, but what if whoever sent it *wants* you to set him free? What do Golems even do when they're free?"

"I don't know!" Naomi cried, pulling out of Eitan's grip so she could pace in little circles, almost exactly like the Golem had. "I don't know who sent it, and I don't know why, and I don't know what's going to happen, and I wish it wasn't happening to me!" she yelled. "But we have to do *something*!"

"So . . . we don't set him free?" Becca asked tentatively.

"*No*," Naomi told her. "I can't just release him into the wild like a cheetah or something, Becks. He needs something to do. He needs a *purpose*. You saw what happened before. And he's even bigger now; who knows what would happen."

"Okay," Eitan said slowly, "so you can't let him go without giving him something to do. So just give him something to do."

"What?" Naomi stopped pacing so she could look at him.

Eitan pulled out the little notebook in which he had been tracking the Golem's progress. "Look, you're right. We want answers, but we don't have any, and we have a problem right now." He pointed at the paper. "Golems need a task." He pointed at Naomi's Golem. "*He* definitely needs a task." He snapped the book shut. "But it seems like anything can be a task if you phrase it correctly, right?"

"Sure," Naomi said, "but if he finishes whatever I tell him to do, he'll just come right back to me."

"So make it something he can't finish." Becca was nodding slowly, like she did when she had just had a big idea. "Something massive. That way you're still in charge, not whatever creeper sent him, but he's out of your way."

Naomi bit her lip. "Like what?"

"Something good," Becca suggested. "Something that *helps*."

"He's here to help," Eitan reminded them. He sounded only a little sarcastic, so Naomi didn't pinch him.

"Okay." Naomi turned to look at the Golem.

"So something big, that helps. There are enough of those, right?"

Eitan sighed. "There's nothing *but* big problems, really."

Naomi matched his sigh with one of her own. She was feeling better with her friends there, thinking of a plan. There were very few things that Becca's thinking face and Eitan's notebook couldn't solve together. "I mean, sure." She thought of her mama and all the lectures about the world's problems. "I can't exactly tell the Golem to go smash the patriarchy, though. He only does actual, physical smashing."

"So we think of actual, physical problems," Eitan said.

"Gun violence," Becca supplied.

"Homelessness," Eitan chimed in.

"Wildfires."

"Preserving the wilderness."

"Health care."

Eitan snorted. "I don't think the Golem can help with that, Becks."

Becca shrugged. "Dad says it's a big problem, and we're brainstorming."

"All right," Naomi said, holding up her hands.

"I think we get the idea." She turned away from her friends to focus on the Golem where he stood at her hip, poised and ready for action. "Golem," she said carefully, turning her words over in her mind before speaking, "I have a task for you." The Golem's calm waiting immediately became more alert and alive, though it didn't move. "I want you to help the world. To make it better." Naomi paused, thinking. "There are a lot of problems, and someone like you could make a big difference. You could fix a lot of things. That's what I want you to do. The kinds of things they said: gun violence, homelessness, protecting the wilderness. Do things that help, and keep helping. You can't come back. Not until everything is fixed."

The Golem didn't move for a moment, and Naomi held her breath, certain that she had somehow done something wrong. Then she blinked, and the Golem was gone. His glowing footsteps traced a blurred path to the tree line and beyond. Naomi felt that now-familiar charge of magic in the air that settled onto her skin like pins and needles. In the dark, eyes and teeth flickered in the corner of her vision as the whispers grew louder for a moment and then faded like they were following the Golem away. She blinked rapidly, trying to clear her head. This was for the best, she told herself. If the voices were gone, that was a good sign. Whatever weird energy it was that followed the Golem and drew those things to her, Naomi didn't want anything to do with it.

"Holy smokes," Becca whispered. She stood on her tiptoes, looking around the edges of the park for where the Golem could have gone. Naomi remembered that Becca couldn't see the footprints, so she couldn't see the path he had taken.

Eitan let out a breath. "Is that it?"

Naomi looked over at her friends. "That's it." She was crying again. "I hope he'll be okay." Eitan slung an arm around her shoulder, and Becca fell into step on Naomi's other side.

"He's a freakishly fast magical gingerbread man, and you were very clear with your instructions," Becca said. "Nothing's going to happen to him."

They walked arm in arm to the bike racks, Naomi sniffling between them. When they released one another to go their respective ways, Naomi suddenly remembered something. "Oh, Eitan!

You're going to have to bake a cake for Cantor Debbie."

Naomi made it home on her bike just as her phone started to ring. "I'm here, Mom!" she called. She skidded into the kitchen, barely stopping herself from crashing against the counter, and tried to catch her breath. Her mom put her cell phone down, and the buzzing in Naomi's pocket stopped.

"Just in time, Nomes!" her mama called. "Will you help Deena bring the pizza over?" Deena held up the big ceramic plates of now-finished pizza—one with mushrooms and spinach for Deena and Mom, one with peppers and onions for Naomi and Mama—and Naomi went over to take one from her and carry it to the coffee table. She squished herself between her moms on the couch before Deena could claim the middle spot, burying her face into her mama's shoulder and breathing in the incense and disinfectant smell of her. She always smelled like that after she'd been teaching. The scent was familiar and soothing for Naomi's frazzled nerves. Mama put a soft hand on her hair, gently teasing through the dense curls. "You okay, baby?" Naomi shook her head, keeping her face pressed against her mama's side. "Did something happen with Eitan?" Naomi shook her head again. "Do you want to talk about it?"

Naomi took a deep, shuddering breath. "No."

"Okay." Her mama was very good about letting her decide when to talk about things. Naomi could almost feel the look Mom was giving Mama over the top of her head, but it didn't matter. It was a house rule; if Naomi said she wasn't ready to talk about it, they would leave it alone, even if Mom was desperately nosy.

The couch jostled as Deena threw herself down beside Mom. "What's wrong with the munchkin?"

Naomi kicked out at her without any real aim and felt her mom's hand come up to catch her ankle and return her foot to the floor. "Just a tough night, Deens," Mama said. "We're not talking about it. Are we ready to start the movie?"

Deena hit play, and the bright musical notes of the beginning of whatever classic movie her mom had picked for the night filled the dark living

6

MYSTERIOUS
HAPPENINGS

Naomi was at Becca's when the first news broke. It had been only a couple of days, but really, she should have known. Her skin had been itching in that same pins-and-needles way it did whenever some of the Golem's strange magic was happening around her. She hadn't had any more demon encounters since she had sent the Golem away, but every once in a while there was a prickle of *something*.

Even without the feeling of magic in the air, Naomi could tell that there was news. Sirens had been screaming past the neighborhood all afternoon, but Mrs. Reznik was ignoring it in the practiced way of a mother of four unruly children on winter break. They didn't know the cause of the commotion until Mr. Reznik burst in after work in his usual boisterous way. He was immediately mobbed by the three younger Reznik siblings, all of them screaming. Unfazed, he swept Benji and Ariela up in each arm while Jake leaped up and clung to his back like a monkey. "Sarah!" he called, tromping slowly toward the kitchen, weighed down by children, "I think there are more kids in this family now than when I left this morning."

Becca's mom looked up from where she was working at her laptop at the counter and nodded toward where Becca and Naomi were sorting Becca's maps. "Just the one extra," she said mildly.

"Hmm," Mr. Reznik rumbled. "Well, I suppose if it's just the one." He deposited the twins on the kitchen floor and detached Jake from around his neck. "Did you hear?"

"Hear what?" Mrs. Reznik asked.

Naomi and Becca perked up. Mr. Reznik worked at the local newspaper, and he always had important news before everyone else. Sure enough, he knew what the sirens were about.

"Something like twenty guns and ammo shops were robbed today around the city," he told them. "Cleared clean out, and the clerks didn't see a thing. The police are worried it's a gang thing, someone's arming up for something big."

Mrs. Reznik cast a meaningful glance at the assorted children in the kitchen, but Mr. Reznik just shrugged. "They know about guns already, Sarah."

She sighed but didn't protest. Becca and Naomi shared a significant look. "Yeah, Mom," Becca said coolly, "we had a drill the last week of school before break, remember." This made Mrs. Reznik sigh again, this time with more of an edge to it, but again, she stayed silent.

"They don't know who did it?" Naomi asked.

"No clue," Mr. Reznik said. "A source told the crime guy at the paper that there was a strange reddish blur caught on some of the cameras, but other than that they've got nothing." He jostled Jake, who was determinedly trying to regain his place on his dad's back but was too short to do much but wrinkle Mr. Reznik's dress shirt. "Maybe it's that superhero from those comics of yours." He mimed zooming around with his hand. "*Whoosh*, in and out in a red blur."

Jake rolled his eyes. "The Flash doesn't live in L.A., Dad. He lives in Star City. *Duh.*"

Mr. Reznik laughed. "My bad, son. Must be some other superhero, then."

Becca nudged Naomi, and Naomi nodded, her stomach churning. She didn't tell Becca that she was already certain it was the Golem. That was a conversation that needed to happen for real, not in nudges and significant looks. Besides, they only knew of one thing that could move so fast it looked like a smudgy blur of reddish brown in the air; it wasn't like Naomi's weird Golem sense gave them any more information than plain old deductive reasoning. Under the table, Naomi sent a text to their Best Friends chat: **Guys. Gun violence.**

The next time something happened, Naomi was home alone trying to get to the next level in the overly violent video game her grandma had given her for Hanukkah and her moms hated. She was just gearing up to fight the final boss when her skin started prickling at the same time her phone started screaming with a county-wide alert. *Multiple Silver Alerts*, it said. Naomi had to look up "Silver Alert" on the internet.

"Unexplained or suspicious disappearance of an elderly person, or a person who is developmentally disabled or cognitively impaired," the internet informed her.

Curious, Naomi clicked on the alert for more information. Multiple people had gone missing from a local homeless shelter, the article said, and had done so in a way that the police were classifying as "currently unexplained but being treated as suspicious." The people, the article went on, had been waiting in an overflow area of the shelter to see if there were any open beds to be had. A worker had gone to check something and come back to an empty room, though the only way out was through the lobby the worker had been checking files in, and he was sure no one had walked by. Naomi felt her heart rising into her throat as she read the words "Many of the people in question suffer from serious mental illness, while others are reported to be elderly and easily confused. The only evidence currently available is another shelter patron's report that they witnessed a blurred red shape go in and out of the room. Police are currently denying any connection to the munitions thefts from the day before, where witnesses also reported seeing a blur of red on the security camera before discovering that merchandise was missing. Police had no comment regarding other reported disappearances of homeless individuals from various encampments and highly trafficked parks across the city."

With a shaking hand, she closed out of the article and pulled up her messages. Eitan had beaten her to the punch this time. **Homelessness.** He had included a link to the article Naomi had just been reading.

Holy smokes, Becca had responded. **You don't think he'll hurt those people?**

Naomi shook her head violently, even though no one was around to see her. **He wouldn't,** she replied. **He's helping.**

Sure, but is he? Becca was always the skeptic. Sometimes Naomi was grateful for her rational, regulated worldview. Now was not one of those times. **Where do you think he took them?**

I bet if we keep an eye on the news, we'll find out, Eitan replied, practical as ever.

They did.

It took very little time for the news to break that the missing people had been found in an unopened hotel that was going up in a neighborhood close to the shelter. Someone had filled the dining room with nonperishable prepacked meals and toiletries. The police had raided the place after a jogger had reported lights in the windows, and the people were evicted. The article didn't mention what had happened to all the people after that. Naomi wondered if they had been arrested.

She sent Eitan the link. She couldn't deal with Becca's particular brand of "told you so" just then. He video-called her immediately.

"Holy heck, Nae," he breathed into the phone, too close to the camera as always.

"What's going to happen to all those people?" Naomi asked miserably.

Eitan was quiet for a very long moment. "My dad says they'll probably be held in jail overnight, but most likely they're just back on the street or at the shelter. Unless the hotel owner decides he wants to be really aggressive about pressing charges." He sighed. "Maybe ask your mom, though. Dad doesn't do that kind of law, you know."

Naomi scrubbed at her eyes. "This doesn't feel like helping."

"I know, Nae, but what can you do? You were really specific. I don't think me or Becca could have said it better. And you told him not to come back." He shrugged, jostling the phone a bit. He was chewing his nail again. "He's probably just doing his best to follow directions."

Before Naomi could answer, there was a beep on the line. Naomi sighed. "I'm going to conference Becca in," she warned.

Becca was already talking when Naomi answered. "—know you guys are talking without me, which is totally rude."

"Hey, Becks," Eitan said tiredly. "Have anything useful to add?"

"Do you think the Golem is, like, *enormous* by now?" She was breathless and speaking fast, clearly more excited than worried. Naomi choked on a sob.

Eitan made a frustrated noise. "Becca! That's not helpful!"

"I'm just saying, he's been doing *a lot* of big things. What if he's bigger than a house? Or a rocket ship! What happens to us if the Golem gets big enough to affect Earth's gravity?"

"Since when are you so on board with the Golem's magical stuff anyway?" Eitan demanded, trying to make significant faces at Becca without Naomi noticing, which was a difficult thing to do on a group video call. "You're the one who said he was just a glorified grabber claw."

"Sure, but I don't ignore evidence that's right in front of me, Eitan," Becca said scornfully. "That would be irresponsible. If it does stuff, it grows. I've seen it with my own eyes." She finally caught on to Eitan's frantic eyebrow signals and sighed. "Look, Nae, I know you're, like, freaking out, but let's be honest. The guns going missing? That's more good than harm, without a doubt. I bet he just totally, like, *boom*, dusted them. And all those people who got busted, that sucks, I totally agree, but they had a night of clean beds and food and showers, and my mom says that some people actually try to get arrested so they get fed and have a place to sleep, so . . ." She trailed off a bit at their silence. "I'm just saying, I know it's not your big grand visions of a better world, but he's doing more good than harm, right? It's probably not some evil plan in action. He's still following your directions."

"That's what I said!" Eitan cried.

"I don't know." Naomi blew out a big breath, trying to stop her voice from shaking. "Maybe. But things are still weird. I thought all the spooky stuff would stop when the Golem left, and it has a little, I guess, but I can still *feel* that stuff is happening, you know? I can feel the Golem, I think, which almost *definitely* means he's gotten a lot bigger. And how can we be sure that he's going to keep doing more good than harm, like you said? You're right, he's going to keep doing big, conspicuous things because I asked him to do big, conspicuous things, and he's going to keep getting bigger, and it's going to be a disaster, and it'll be my fault!" She grabbed the teddy bear on her bed and squeezed it tightly in her fist, digging her nails into the fur until her knuckles were white. "I can't believe how much I messed up! How could we have not thought this through?" She yelled the last question loud enough that Deena banged on the wall to get her to quiet down, but luckily Deena was rarely interested in what Naomi was actually saying to her friends, only that she said it quietly.

"Nae?" Eitan said questioningly. Becca was

silent. When Naomi didn't respond, Eitan tried again. "Naomi—"

She held up her hand, and he stopped. "I think," she said, "that it's way past time we asked for help from someone who knows what they're doing."

Becca's quiet, predictably, couldn't withstand that. "What do you mean, 'someone who knows what they're doing?' You know some Golem expert that you haven't told us about?"

"No," Naomi said, "but think about it. Where are Golems from?"

"Jewish folklore," Eitan said promptly. "Most famously, the Golem of Prague."

"Sure," Naomi said. She had no idea what the Golem of Prague was, because she had not, in fact, read the sheet of notes Eitan had sent her, but she believed that he knew what he was talking about. "Golems are a Jewish creation, so it makes sense we would need someone who knows a lot about being Jewish, right?"

"You don't mean—" Becca said.

"I do," Naomi replied grimly.

"Not on your life," Becca shot back. Naomi set her chin and stared her friend down through the phone screen. Becca blinked first, and Naomi smirked in triumph while Becca fell backward on her bed with a frustrated yell.

"We're doing it," Naomi said.

"Oh jeez," Eitan groaned. "We're going to be in so much trouble." He sighed. "If we do this, we talk totally in hypotheticals, okay? We're doing a school project on folklore, or something." He shrugged. "Maybe Becca's given up her all-consuming passion for maps and has a new special interest." Becca sat back up with a scowl and flicked the screen. Eitan yelped like she'd actually hit him. "I'm just saying! At best, he'll think we're nuts. At worst, he'll call our parents!" Becca and Naomi shuddered in unison, and Eitan nodded grimly. "Right. So. Hypotheticals."

"Hypotheticals," Naomi agreed. Becca nodded.

Eitan let out a long breath. "Fine. All right, who has B'nei Mitzvah prep next?"

"I'm going tomorrow," Becca said.

Naomi tightened her grip on her teddy bear and nodded decisively. "Great. We'll all go with you. We'll tell our parents we want to practice our prayers in the sanctuary or something."

"We're really going to talk to Rabbi Levinson

about this?" Becca asked, like maybe Naomi was talking about a *different* expert on Jewish things they all knew, or maybe more like she thought Naomi would change her mind if she sounded doubtful enough.

"Yes," Naomi said. "We have to. We're officially out of our depth."

"Well," Eitan said, sounding like a man walking to his execution. "If the rabbi can't figure out a way to fix it, we'll know it's hopeless, and we'll just have to move to Antarctica and change our names and hope the Golem and all the weird creepy magic happening around him follows us there, where there aren't actually any people to notice."

"Thanks, Eitan," Naomi said.

"Just being realistic."

Becca snorted. "Super-reasonable backup plan, dude. All right. Tomorrow morning, we talk to the rabbi."

"Tomorrow morning, we talk to the rabbi," Naomi agreed.

7

TEMPLE BETH TORAH

Becca's mom dropped them off at the front of the temple instead of the side like Naomi's mom usually did, which meant they got to push open the wide double doors with the fancy carved handles and enter together into the echoing, empty lobby. Entering the temple that way always made Naomi feel very dramatic, but the familiar feel and smell of the lobby was like a comforting blanket that wrapped itself around her shoulders the moment she stepped through the doors. She thought sometimes that she would be able to map the layout of the building in her mind for the rest of her life, even if she never went back. Soft, warm light and dark wood paneling led the way to the sanctuary, where the echoes of the ceramic-tiled lobby were muffled by cushioned pews and threadbare carpets, and the air was dusty-sweet with the smell of old books and older Torah scrolls. If she turned the other way, a door opened off the atrium like a portal, revealing white linoleum and a hallway full of fluorescent light. Naomi had squeaked her way down those shiny, disinfectant-smelling halls for Hebrew school every Sunday for most of her life. Naomi and Eitan sent Becca off down the fluorescent-filled hall toward the administrative offices where the rabbi held his meetings, then turned toward the sanctuary. It would be busy later—the older kids had their Hebrew school classes on Wednesday evenings—but at this time of day, the temple was empty.

Naomi threw herself backward into a pew, careful of her shoes against the old, polished wood of the arm, trying to make her jittery nerves calm down. She had never seen any of the whispery shadows in the sanctuary before sundown, thankfully, and the normal silence of the temple on a weekday morning seemed to be just that:

normal. She breathed out slowly and tried to relax. It didn't really work. "We're going to be in so much trouble," she said.

Eitan's face loomed over her. "We're not even telling him what's happening."

"He's going to see right through us, and *then* we'll be in so much trouble."

"Well, yeah, probably. I've been telling you that all morning."

"I should listen to you more."

"I've been telling you *that* for ten years."

Naomi groaned and sat up. "It's worth it to try, though, isn't it? Rabbi Levinson has got to know something, right?"

Eitan patted her shoulder. "Rabbi Levinson knows everything."

It was true enough. Naomi had never seen Rabbi Levinson stumped by a question. There was even a game a few of the temple members liked to play at the High Holidays called 'Stump the Rabbi.' Naomi's mama said it was obnoxious, and her mom had some harsher opinions about the time wasted on those questions on Yom Kippur, when they always ended services late anyway and "people are *hungry*, Bob; no one cares about your contrived thought exercise," but some people spent the whole year trying to think of particularly thorny questions. As far back as Naomi could remember, the rabbi had answered all of them without blinking. She sighed. "Let's hope he knows this."

Eventually, Becca finished her lesson and summoned the two of them through the linoleum portal to the rabbi's office, where they squished onto the giant beanbag and stared at him, trying to think of how to begin. The rabbi leaned back in his chair and watched them watch him, as patient as he always was with their antics. His yarmulke today was dark purple with little gold moons and stars embroidered on it, and he was wearing a tie to match. It didn't make it any easier to meet his concerned, well-meaning eyes.

Naomi squirmed in the silence until she couldn't take it anymore. Then she took a piece of candy from the little glass bowl on the desk and crunched down hard on it, ignoring Eitan's wince beside her.

"Okay," she said, pushing the shards of candy around her cheeks and trying to remember how to breathe in a way that didn't make her seem suspicious. "We have a hypothetical question for you, and it sounds silly, but it's really important, okay?"

Rabbi Levinson frowned. "Is everything okay?"

"Yeah, totally," Naomi said. "Completely. Everything's very normal. The situation is totally hypothetical." Eitan shifted a little next to her like he wanted to step on her foot and stop her babbling but couldn't figure out how to do it on the beanbag without Rabbi Levinson noticing. Naomi ignored him. "Hypothetical," she repeated, "but it is important, and we need a serious answer."

The rabbi held up a hand like a Boy Scout. "I promise to be serious."

"And it would also be really nice if you would promise not to ask us any other questions about it, either," Becca added. Eitan gave up on being subtle and leaned across Naomi to pinch her. Becca glared.

Rabbi Levinson huffed a small laugh, though his frown got deeper almost immediately. "That one may depend more on what it is you're here to tell me, Rebecca, but I'll do my best."

Naomi looked at her friends. Eitan gave her a

tight little nod. Becca shrugged noncommittally. That was as much support as Naomi was going to get, probably. "Okay," she said. "So, we've been reading about Golems, and we were wondering, if a Golem got too big, like in the stories"—she had finally read some of Eitan's notes to prepare for meeting with the rabbi—"and then got away and was free in a city, how would you find it and catch it again? Hypothetically."

There was a long moment in which Rabbi Levinson stared at them silently. Then he pulled his glasses off his face and dug the heels of his hands into his eyes like he was trying to wake himself up. He replaced his glasses, blinked at them some more, took a piece of candy from the bowl and crunched down on it even more ferociously than Naomi had, and said, "Okay, explain that to me."

They did so in a confusion of overlapping voices, shouting one another down whenever anyone veered too far from the agreed-upon version of the story and risked making their cover story even more flimsy than it already was and talking over one another until the rabbi held up his hands for silence. "That is a very interesting

hypothetical," he said, "and a complicated one."
He pressed his fingertips together and rested his
chin on top of his hands, looking at them con-
sideringly. "I think that this is a discussion that
will require more serious fortification than the
candy bowl can provide," he told them finally.
"Wait here." He pushed back from the desk and
left the office, leaving the three of them stunned
and blinking.

"Do you think he's going to get beer?" Becca
whispered.

Eitan shot her a dark look. "Don't be absurd,
Becks. He's the *rabbi*, and we're at *temple*."

Becca shrugged. "I'm just saying, whenever my
dad says a conversation is going to require fortification, he gets a beer."

"He's not getting beer, Becca," Naomi hissed,
then, at the sound of footsteps squeaking back
down the hall toward them, said, "Shut up!"

They all sat up at attention when the rabbi
came back in, holding a box of Girl Scout cookies. He shot them a bemused expression but
didn't comment on their sudden, overly keen
interest in good posture. They watched him as he
sat back down and opened the box, tossing one

sleeve of Thin Mints to Naomi and opening the other. He ate three cookies right in a row faster than Eitan ate toaster pastries, and then he said, "So, I think we should start with the Golem of Prague."

8

THE GOLEM OF
PRAGUE

In Prague, many years ago, long before even your grandparents were born, there was a lot of negative feeling toward the Jews.

Becca snorted and muttered, "What else is new?" and Eitan reached around Naomi again to poke her in the side. Rabbi Levinson ignored them and went on with his story.

People who wanted to hurt the Jewish community would tell lies about how the Jews killed non-Jewish children and used their blood to make their matzah.

"Gross."

"Shh, Becca."

One day, the rabbi decided he had had enough. He prayed to God to help him protect the Jewish people from the deadly lies, and God told him what to do. The rabbi built a man out of mud and clay and spoke a holy word over it, and it came to life. "Your purpose is to help protect the Jewish people from these dangerous lies," the rabbi told the Golem, for that's what he had made. He took the Golem home and showed his wife. He told his wife that this Golem had a divine purpose and should not be used for easy tasks. Then the rabbi sent the Golem to guard the gates of the Jewish quarter, to be sure no one who wanted to make mischief against the Jews came through. The Golem did so, then returned to the rabbi for its next task.

The rabbi went to speak to the people, to decide the best thing the Golem could do. While he was gone, his wife, who worked very hard all day to keep their home and care for the community, asked the Golem to fetch some water from the well. The Golem did so, but the rabbi's wife soon realized her mistake. You see, the Golem was so intent in its purpose that it couldn't stop fetching water, though the barrels were overflowing, the kettle was full, and the trough for the animals was pouring water into the dirt like a spout. The rabbi came home and saw what had happened and laughed. "A fine job fetching water, but I have another task for you, Golem, one more suited to you." He took the Golem back to the gates and sent it to patrol the walls of the ghetto, to be sure that no one was plotting anything.

So it was that that night a man who owed some money to a Jewish butcher had come up with an evil plan, so that he wouldn't have to repay his debt. He kidnapped his sister's son and left him in a basement, then went to the police and told them that the butcher was responsible for the boy's disappearance. The butcher was brought to trial and would have been sentenced to death on just the greedy man's word—that's just how things went back then—when the Golem burst into the courthouse with the boy in its arms, and the boy shouted out for everyone to hear, "Uncle! Uncle! Why did you leave me locked in that room?"

Rabbi Levinson smiled at their shocked gasps. "Crazy stuff, right?" They nodded.

The judge saw the lie for what it was and immediately met with the rabbi about the lies that were told all too often about the Jewish residents of the city. The judge agreed that such cases accusing Jews of harming non-Jewish children without any proof of wrongdoing would no longer be heard. The rabbi celebrated. The Golem, its purpose fulfilled, was brought into the attic of the temple, where the rabbi spoke more holy words and turned the Golem back into clay. It is said that the Golem is still hidden somewhere in Prague, waiting to be used again, should we need it.

Naomi chewed thoughtfully on a Thin Mint, swatting Eitan away when he tried to grab another one. "You have three in your hand," she told him. She turned back to the rabbi. "That doesn't sound very much like our Golem," she said. Becca elbowed her. "Our hypothetical Golem," she said quickly, "which we're researching for a project."

The rabbi inclined his head. "It's true, there are some pretty major differences in the story of the Golem of Prague compared to this contemporary Golem story you've stumbled across. I'd love to read it sometime, if you'll email me a copy." The girls turned to Eitan, who smiled nervously. There was chocolate on his teeth.

"Sure," he said. "I'll try to remember."

Rabbi Levinson grinned at him. "Awesome. Okay, like you said, it's pretty different. *But* there are some parts that seem to me to be close enough to be starting off with." He pointed at Eitan with his cookie. "Show me that list of yours." He took the notebook from Eitan and glanced through it, stopping at certain pages or turning back to look at whatever Eitan had written at earlier points. "This is very thorough," he said approvingly. "Okay, so there are a lot of Golem stories, dating back to early rabbinical times. There are similar themes in all of them, but no two stories are the same. The Golem of Prague is the most famous, but that doesn't necessarily mean it's the most true." He tapped on a bit of writing that Naomi couldn't make out from where she sat. "Common threads of all these stories are that the Golem can't speak"—he mimed a check mark in the air over the notebook—"that they sometimes overdo tasks so that things stop being helpful." Rabbi Levinson wiggled his hand side to side in a gesture that he made often. As far as Naomi could tell, it meant "eh."

"You could say that the Golem in your story has gotten near that point, but from what you've said, there hasn't been any incident like the water-fetching."

"So far," muttered Eitan.

The rabbi looked up from the notebook. "What was that?"

"Nothing, never mind."

The rabbi shrugged. "Okay. Well, there are also some stories that talk about Golems growing larger and more difficult to control as they're given more tasks." He mimed another check mark, then ate another cookie, nodding to himself.

"What about other . . . weird stuff . . . happening around the Golem?" Naomi asked.

"Weird stuff?" the rabbi echoed. "Weird in what way?"

Naomi fidgeted with her fingers. "I'm not sure. Like . . . seeing and hearing strange things. Ghosts, maybe, or demons. I keep, um, reading stories. And they said that people around the Golem start meeting other people who don't really seem like real . . . people," she finished lamely. She wasn't sure how to explain that being around the Golem had somehow made her see demons and sense the presence of ghosts and other things Naomi was certain she never wanted to see. It didn't seem like "Is magic contagious?" was a question the rabbi would have the answer to, without having a lot more questions of his own. Naomi wasn't even sure *magic* was the right word. None of it *felt* like the magic in storybooks was supposed to feel. "Like if there were ghosts in the temple," she said quietly, "and people who'd been around the Golem could see them."

Instead of giving her a weird look or telling her she was talking crazy like Naomi thought he would, the rabbi looked thoughtful. "Huh," he said. "Well, that's not the most unbelievable thing I've ever heard."

"It's not?" Becca asked.

"I hear a lot of unbelievable things as a rabbi, you know." He tapped the side of his nose like Naomi had seen her grandfather do when he had a secret. "As it is, I've never heard anything about Golems bestowing magical senses on people near them, but ghosts in a synagogue. Well." He smiled. "Synagogues are interesting spaces, full of history. There are all sorts of folktales about ghostly congregants and sometimes even demons worshipping in synagogues in their own way. I'll give you guys a book."

Eitan sat up straighter, looking pleased. Becca seemed less happy about it. "A book?" she said doubtfully. "You're giving us homework?"

"I'm giving you research," he corrected her. "For your research project that you clearly care about very much. It never hurts to learn more." He got up and pulled a thick hardcover book from his shelf and passed it over his desk to Naomi. She took it, running her fingers over the rich colors and patterns of the cover.

"That's true," Naomi allowed. They were very out of their depth, and she wasn't about to turn down new information. "But what about—" She stopped, afraid to ask the question she was worried she already knew the answer to.

Eitan did it for her. "How did people stop the Golems in the stories?"

Rabbi Levinson took his glasses off to rub his eyes and sighed. Then he pushed the remainder of his sleeve of cookies across the table toward them. Nobody took one. The rabbi gave them another odd look, like he didn't quite believe that everything really was okay. "Well, like I said, I don't know about this . . . residual magic you're talking about. Try to remember to email me those stories, Eitan. They sound very interesting. But in every story I've heard, the Golem has to be destroyed before it can cause too much damage." Naomi bit down on her lips so they wouldn't tremble and waited for Rabbi Levinson to go on. "Except for the Golem of Prague, most of the stories about Golems are lessons about how the power of creation is meant for God alone. That's why they can never speak, because only God can grant that ability."

"What about the Prague Golem?" Becca asked.

"God gave the rabbi the idea that time," Naomi said, before the rabbi could respond.

Rabbi Levinson nodded. "And even then, the Golem didn't stay alive to keep helping. It fulfilled its purpose, and then it was done."

Naomi reached for another cookie for something to do with her hands, then put it down again. Her stomach was queasy. "So they had to kill the Golems?"

The rabbi hesitated. "Well, *kill* is a strong term."

"Is it?" Naomi demanded, feeling her voice go

high-pitched and tight. "Golems aren't dolls or toys. They might not be fully alive, but they're more than just statues. They're *real*, and they're trying to fulfill a purpose someone gave them, and they killed them!"

Eitan cleared his throat. Becca looked uncomfortable. Naomi took a shaky breath. "Sorry," she said. "I'm just really . . . invested in this project."

"Naomi." Rabbi Levinson looked worried. "Are you sure everything's all right?"

"Yes!" Eitan nearly shouted. The rabbi looked a little surprised at the forcefulness of it.

"Naomi?"

Naomi shook her head. "I'm fine. I'm sorry. Like I said, I'm just really invested. It feels like we've read so many stories that the Golems are real to us now." She tried to smile. There was no reason to lose it and make the rabbi suspicious. Any new information was a place to start, she reminded herself. Anything the rabbi told them could only help, and if they had a plan, they could go after the Golem. She knew she could find him. Even after several days, Naomi could see the glowing trail of the Golem's path out of the corner of her eye whenever she passed by the park. She knew if they could figure out where he had last been, she could track him down. "Please, Rabbi Levinson, is there anything else you can tell us?"

Rabbi Levinson made a face like he had a terrible headache. Naomi thought he probably did. He definitely hadn't expected to be ambushed in his office about Golems. "I can do some more reading," he offered.

Naomi nodded. "Thank you."

The rabbi gave her a look like he knew exactly what she was hiding and was choosing to let her keep her secrets. Naomi shoved her hands under her knees and leaned forward, putting on the most innocent face she could manage. "We're very excited about this project, Rabbi Levinson, and we *super* appreciate your help!"

The rabbi held her gaze for a long moment until, finally, he sighed and leaned back. "You're welcome anytime," he said. "I'm always happy to answer questions and help with projects—you guys know that."

The three of them nodded rapidly. "We know!"

Rabbi Levinson nodded. "Okay, go. I've got three more meetings before lunch, and as much as I have enjoyed our chat, I can't spend the whole day discussing hypothetical Golems." He smiled at them. "I'll send Eitan a list of books."

They nodded some more and said some more "thank you"s, then pushed at one another until they all managed to clamber off the beanbag and tumble out of the office into the quiet of the hallway. They exchanged looks, and Naomi said quietly, "Outside." They went.

9

AN ADVENTURE BEGINS

"Now what?" asked Becca.

Naomi rubbed her eyes. "You heard the rabbi. It's not going to stop on its own. We have to go after it."

"Oh God," Eitan groaned. "The rabbi. We lied to the rabbi! Oh, this is so much worse than lying about cake, Nae. We're going to be *toast* for this one. Can't we just leave the Golem alone? It's not your fault he didn't come with good instructions. Maybe the person who sent him to you wanted *you* to get in trouble."

"It doesn't matter if I didn't know. I gave him

the task. I have a responsibility. Are you with me?" Becca and Eitan shared a look.

"Of course, Nae," Eitan said. "I was just saying."

"Thank you," Naomi said. She pulled out her phone to check the time. It was still early, barely noon. "Okay, here's the plan."

Becca's mom picked them up from the temple and took them each back to their own house. Then it was just a matter of waiting. Naomi's moms were leaving in the afternoon for some pre–New Year's Eve work event that her mom's office was holding. Those events always ran late into the night, which meant Deena was in charge. That made it easy. As soon as the door shut behind her parents, Naomi bounded up the stairs and banged on the wall. "Deens, I'm going to sleep at Becca's, okay?" Naomi yelled.

Deena stuck her head out of her room. "Did you tell the Mothership?"

"Yeah. They said it's fine."

Naomi watched as her sister weighed the possibility of getting out of babysitting with the possibility of being in trouble if she didn't double-check.

But Naomi knew for a fact that Deena's friends were going to the movies that night, and Deena really wanted to go with them. "All right," she said. "Whatever. You need a ride?"

"Nope!" Naomi told her. "I'm gonna bike."

"Cool." Deena disappeared back into her room, and Naomi waited until her door clicked shut before darting into her own room and closing the door firmly behind her. She swiped her backpack from her bed and began filling it with snacks, a flashlight, a toothbrush, and the thirty-six dollars Eitan had given her, plus the forty dollars from her piggy bank. She grabbed her warmest sweatshirt and a battery pack for her phone, double-checked everything, and decided she was ready. She slammed back down the stairs, ignoring Deena's yell to "stop acting like an elephant," and raced out the door, barely slowing down to grab her bike before she was running down the street with it and jumping on.

She made it to the park in record time. Becca and Eitan pulled up alongside her as she rolled her bike onto the dirt path that cut around the swing set. Becca had her tube of maps under her arm, and Eitan's backpack in his bike basket was overflowing with what looked like a whole library's worth of research and notes. Beyond the swings, Naomi could see the Golem's footprints, which snaked in a glowing trail into the trees and across the path that led deeper into the park. "Everyone covered?" she asked.

Becca wiggled her fingers in the air. "I told my parents I was staying at yours."

"Same," Eitan said.

"I told Deena I was at yours." She nodded at Becca. "And no one will bother checking because Deena's supposed to be in charge while my moms are out for the evening."

Eitan pushed his too-big helmet back from his forehead and grinned. "Deena's going to be so grounded if they find out."

Naomi shook her head, sighing. "Deena never stays grounded. Mama says that teenage rebellion is a natural part of her learning to be independent and that Mom should forgive her for being irresponsible sometimes."

Becca mimed puking on the ground. "My mom says that being grounded builds character and shows the siblings that actions have consequences."

"Well, not everyone's mom can be a hippie," Eitan reasoned. "And Naomi was more likely to get a hippie mom because she has two of them. The odds are better."

Naomi rolled her eyes. "Okay, guys, focus. Golem to find, world to save—sound familiar?" They nodded. Becca reached over and tightened Eitan's helmet strap for him. Naomi watched Becca secure her own helmet and nodded back. "Perfect. Let's go."

She hefted her backpack and swung her leg over her bike again, setting off after the trail of footprints with Eitan and Becca following close behind.

It felt like any other outing at first. They biked through neighborhoods they had ridden through before and stopped at the bakery that Becca's dad always brought them treats from to stock up on snacks for their ride. Eventually, though, their surroundings turned unfamiliar, and Naomi began to feel the telltale pins and needles over her skin that meant magic was far too close, and getting closer.

"Ugh, my hands fell asleep," Becca grumbled, taking one hand and then the other off the handlebars to shake them out. "I didn't think that was supposed to happen when you're moving around." Eitan shot a quick frown at Becca, his helmet flopping a bit despite the tightened strap as he turned his head quickly back to keep his eyes on the road.

"My arms are prickly too," he called. "Do you think there's some sort of pollen or something making us have allergies?"

Becca scoffed. "I don't have allergies."

Naomi's stomach dropped. "It's not allergies," she said. She pulled her bike over to the side of the road, and her friends followed. She waited until they both climbed off their bikes. Eitan's helmet was back over his eyes.

"Nae?" he asked, tipping his head back to squint at her.

"It's magic," Naomi said. She peered at her friends like she might be able to see the changes on them. Her heart felt like it was crawling into her throat at the same time that her stomach kept swooping downward. Any more bad news and she was pretty sure it would end up in her knees. "The pins-and-needles feeling . . ." She trailed off in the face of Becca's wide-eyed expression. "I'm sorry, guys," she said miserably. "I didn't mean to get you more involved in this mess. Maybe you should just—"

"This is what you've been feeling the *whole time*?" Becca asked. She scrubbed at her arms. "How did you not just . . . scratch yourself out of your skin?"

That made Naomi laugh. Of course Becca would be more worried about crawling skin than weird magical beings. "I'm not as sensitive to that sort of thing as you are, Becks," Naomi reminded her. Becca shuddered theatrically. "Anyway," Naomi went on, comforted by the fact that neither of her friends seemed angry, just a little weirded out, "it's not all the time. Just when something is nearby."

"*Nearby.*"

Naomi looked up at the little huddle of shops they had stopped in front of, scanning the small groups of shoppers that drifted between aisles and along the sidewalks. The barest sound of whispers filtered their way through the back of her mind. Naomi turned her gaze across the street, where a small boy was crouched in front of the gutter like he was looking for something.

Becca and Eitan turned with her, and so they saw when the boy looked up with ink-dark eyes and a too-knowing expression. "Yeah," Naomi whispered, as a woman and a man exited a shop to the right of them and came to a slow stop just out of the corner of her eye. The way their heads tilted in unison made her skin crawl with more urgency and the whispers grow louder and more urgent. "Pretty close, actually."

Eitan's bike bumped against hers as he scooted closer. "The voices . . . Are those . . . ?"

"Part of it?" Naomi said. She held her head as still as possible so that she could keep both the couple and the boy in her line of sight. "Yeah, they are. Are you hearing them now too?" Eitan nodded tightly, and Becca made a little half motion like she was going to grab for Naomi's arm and then stopped herself. Naomi tightened her hold on her handlebars. "We should go."

Her friends didn't need to be told twice. Almost as one, they swung their legs over the seats of their bikes and took off down the street, trying to outrun the whispers and the high, sharp laugh of the boy by the gutter. Naomi followed the Golem's trail, and her friends followed her, and they rode until their goose bumps settled and the only thing Naomi could feel on her skin was the tackiness of her sweat as it cooled in the wind that rushed past her as she rode.

They rode until the neighborhoods and strip malls gave way to more open spaces and wider streets. Then they skirted the edge of the road until they ran up against the high fence of a water treatment plant. Naomi climbed off her bike to peer through the chain links. The Golem's trail disappeared around a building and into a strange cluster of square lakes, then vanished from view. Naomi stood on her tiptoes, craning her neck to see farther past the lakes, but it was no good. She couldn't see where the Golem had gone, or if he had veered off in any direction away from the northward route he had taken so far.

"We need a better view," she muttered. "I need to be able to see." She turned to her friends. "Becks, what's near here that's up high?"

Becca pulled out her maps with an eagerness that Naomi knew meant she had been waiting for this moment. She muttered to herself as she sorted through the maps, then held one in the air in triumph. "Granada Hills and Northward," she announced. She made Eitan turn around and kneel down so she could spread the map across his back—she would rather die than put one of her maps on the ground—and squinted at it. She jabbed at a spot. "Here! The observatory!"

Eitan jumped up so excitedly that Becca's map almost fluttered to the ground. She clutched it against her chest, hissing at Eitan's unapologetic face. "Jonah!" Eitan crowed.

"Jonah?" Naomi asked.

"My cousin Jonah, you remember him? He's in college, and he's an intern at the observatory! He can get us up there!"

"Call him!"

Eitan did. He didn't have to lie very much. Jonah was twenty and interested in stars the way Becca was interested in maps. As soon as Eitan said he and his friends wanted to go up in the observatory, Jonah was on his way. They waited, antsy and impatient, for about half an hour. Fifteen minutes in, Naomi started once again to get that prickly sense on the back of her neck like they were being watched. Beside her, Eitan shivered.

"My dad always says that when you get a chill

like that, it means someone walked over your grave," Becca said.

Eitan shivered again, glaring at her. "Could you not be so creepy, Becks?"

Becca shrugged and didn't answer. Naomi shushed them and moved in closer until she was leaning flush against Eitan's shoulder.

"You guys are still feeling that?"

"Like I've got creepy-crawlies all over me?" Eitan asked. "Yeah. Nae, what do you think it means?"

"That you guys are feeling it now? I'm not sure."

Becca groaned and shifted, pulling at the fabric of her sweatshirt like that was what was making her itchy, even though all of Becca's clothes were carefully selected for texture and weight, and her mom cut the tags out of everything. Nothing was more comfortable than Becca's wardrobe. Naomi reached out and stopped her from pulling her sweatshirt over her head. "It won't help, Becks, and you'll catch cold. I think it must be getting stronger if you guys can feel it too. Back at the strip mall, did you see—"

"The creepiest kid ever and that couple who

looked like they stepped out of a horror movie?" Eitan cut in. "Yeah, I sure did."

Becca nodded in agreement. "Those voices are super creepy, Nae! I can't believe you haven't been having nightmares this whole time!"

"Why now?" Eitan asked.

Naomi thought about it. Up until that day, her friends had seemed oblivious to Naomi's strange encounters. They only knew what to look for because she had told them. "He's much bigger now, probably. Maybe he's pulling you in too, since you're with me so much. Or maybe you can feel it because we're tracking down the Golem now, instead of him just doing things for me," she suggested.

Eitan tapped his chin. "Maybe it's a little bit of both. The Golem's power is stronger, and like . . . we're part of the quest now, for real."

Becca snorted, though Naomi didn't think she sounded like she actually thought anything was very funny. "A quest? You read too much, Eitan."

"We're hunting a Golem and running from creepy supernatural creatures that make us hear voices, Becca! What would you call it?" Becca got a look like she was going to say something snide, but Naomi cut her off.

"One of those supernatural creatures is nearby, guys, and unless arguing about whether or not this ridiculous adventure is a quest is going to somehow bore it to death, we have to figure out something to keep it away."

Eitan immediately pulled out his notebook, shooting a look at Becca that very clearly communicated, *Who reads too much now?* He flipped through it for a few moments, then let out a frustrated breath. "It would be really helpful if Jewish folklore wasn't so inconsistent," he muttered. "No two stories use the same way to get rid of demons!" He shook his head. "I don't suppose we could whip out a cross and see what happens, just in case." He wilted under the combined forces of Naomi's and Becca's withering glares. "Kidding, kidding. Jeez. No one likes a good vampire movie here; I see how it is."

He turned back to his notebook, which was, Naomi knew, really their only hope of any information that could help them deal with whatever was following them. Fortunately, before the tingling sensation of magic creeping up on them got any worse, they were rescued by Eitan's cousin Jonah, who rolled up to the sidewalk in his gray van and honked loudly like they wouldn't know he was there to get them.

10

A TRIP TO
THE OBSERVATORY

The sensation of magic vanished as soon as
Jonah arrived, and all three of the kids breathed
a sigh of relief. If Jonah noticed anything odd
about the way they slumped together at the
sudden loss of tension, he didn't comment, just
waved at them without rolling down the window and gestured at the trunk with a jerk of his
thumb. They loaded their bikes into the large,
flat trunk and scrambled into the van. Jonah
greeted Eitan with a fist bump and the rest of
them with a friendly nod. "'Sup, munchkins. You
trying to see some stars?"

"Oh, definitely," Becca said in her least convincing voice. "Can't get enough stars."

Eitan rolled his eyes. There was a reason Becca was never in charge of their cover story. "Naomi and I are interested in the stars," he told his cousin, "but Becca is actually really into mapping the county. Do you think she could aim the telescope at the ground for a bit to see what's around here?"

Jonah snorted. "Not a chance, bud. We've got those things so precisely calibrated, if you try to move them an inch without permission, you'd mess up years of research."

"Oh."

Jonah glanced around the car at their forlorn faces and cleared his throat uncomfortably. "I mean, that's not to say you can't still have a look!" he said quickly. "I've got a set of binoculars in the car somewhere. You can go out onto the railing and use those. Would that work?" He looked relieved when they all brightened. "Okay, awesome. To the observatory!"

The observatory wasn't much, just a few white, orblike structures on stilts in the middle of a scrubby grass area, but Jonah led them up the ladder into the largest orb, chattering away excitedly about whatever work he was doing there. Naomi had a hard time following what he was saying, but Eitan was making interested noises and nodding along, so she figured that was okay. It was just after dusk, so it wasn't dark enough yet to look at stars. Instead, they crowded out of the main observatory and onto the small external platform to look through Jonah's binoculars at the ground below them. They passed the binoculars around, Eitan taking only a perfunctory glance while Becca panned across the landscape for several minutes, muttering about updating landmarks. Finally, she passed the binoculars over to Naomi, who scanned the ground in the direction they had been heading, looking for some sign of the Golem.

"There!" she shouted, pointing toward a glimmering trail of gold that headed north from where they were. "The trail heads into the mountains!" Becca shushed her and glanced back at Jonah, but he was busy setting up whatever needed setting up inside the small observation space.

"In the mountains," Naomi repeated in a

whisper. "Can Jonah drive us that way?"

Eitan shrugged. "Probably. He's pretty chill. We do have to stay and look at stars, though, or he'll be super bummed."

They stayed until it was just barely dark enough to use the telescopes and saw some early stars, which Naomi had to admit was pretty cool. Becca, even though she had only wanted to look at the ground, seemed awed by it. She hung on Jonah's every word as he explained that they were basically making a detailed map of the sky and asked questions about star maps and their relation to the earth. Then Jonah needed to get to his actual work. "Do you guys need a ride home?" he asked, jotting down some notes on his laptop. "I can drop you real fast."

"Actually," Eitan said, "would you be willing to drop us off somewhere in Santa Clarita?"

Jonah looked up, frowning. "What's in Santa Clarita?"

"The Chabad house!" Becca blurted out. Eitan and Naomi sent her bewildered looks, but she pushed on. "My aunt Ruth is, um, making dinner there, and she, um, she wanted us to come. Because my parents are ordering pizza for the siblings and"—she looked wildly at Naomi—"Naomi's allergic to cheese!"

Naomi glared at Becca from behind Jonah's back, trying to communicate how crazy Becca sounded, but Jonah only shrugged. "That's cool of her," he said. He checked his watch and grimaced. "That's not close, though, and I have to get these images at really specific times." His face pinched with indecision. Naomi could tell he was about to suggest calling a parent.

"It's fine," she said quickly. "We can bike part of the way and then"—she winced at the terrible lie—"Becca's aunt Ruth can come meet us. Don't worry about it, Jonah. Thanks for the, uh, stars and stuff."

The other two thanked Jonah as well, Eitan receiving another fist bump and a demand that he text when they got where they're going, and they trooped back down the stairs to their bikes.

"Ugh, Santa Clarita is so far from here," Becca complained as they strapped their helmets on. "Are you sure Jonah can't take us part of the way?"

"He has a job to do here, Becks," Eitan reminded her. "He could maybe take us, like, fifteen minutes out, but then he'd want to call our parents. He's a dumb college kid, but he's not *stupid*. He won't just leave us in the middle of the road without telling anyone."

"Well, I think—" Becca started. Naomi kicked off and rode in the direction of the Golem, and whatever it was Becca thought was lost in the wind. She did hear the cry of indignation behind her, but she ignored it. Her friends caught up easily enough, and they rode through the falling darkness until they came back to real roads still busy with the ever-present bottleneck of cars.

Finally, they had to admit defeat. The Golem's trail was still clear, but they knew better than to ride their bikes at night in LA traffic. Naomi pulled her bike to the side of the road, pushing her helmet back to wipe the sweat from her forehead. "We better stop. Becca?" she said. Becca nodded and pulled out her phone. Eitan swung his helmet idly as they waited, clacking it against Naomi's handlebars and sticking his tongue out at her when she shot him a dirty look. Eventually, Becca made a sound of triumph.

"You guys are never going to believe this, but there's a synagogue, like, four blocks from here."

Eitan looked skeptical. "How does that help? They won't let us sleep in a synagogue," he said doubtfully. "Would they?"

"No," Becca admitted, "probably not, but we don't have to ask them. We just sneak in."

Naomi had her doubts about that, but it was true that they didn't have very many options.

"Come on," Becca said. "It'll be safe there, and the pews are bound to be comfy enough to crash on for a night. They might even have a nap room for the preschoolers like our temple does. We just have to get in before they close and then hide somewhere until everyone's gone."

Eitan still looked doubtful, and Becca let out a frustrated noise. "Do you have a better idea?"

Slowly, Eitan shook his head. "I guess not."

"Great. Nae?"

Naomi took a deep breath. She was tired and scared. She didn't know what they were doing. All she really wanted was to call her mama to come get her and take her home. But the Golem was hers, and he was out there alone. She had a responsibility. "Let's do it."

11

A GHOSTLY
CONGREGATION

They made it just in time for the evening Hebrew school classes to be letting out. It was surprisingly easy for them to blend in with the crowd of other kids milling around on the sidewalk and in the lobby waiting for pickup, even as dirty and sweaty from biking as they were. They parked their bikes around the corner so they wouldn't be noticed on the racks by the front door by anyone leaving late at night and slipped inside.

Naomi immediately felt better. The inside of this temple had the same smell of disinfectant and candle wax as her own temple, and the softly glowing lights mounted on the warm sand-brown walls of the sanctuary felt familiar and welcoming. "Where should we hide?" she whispered. It probably wasn't necessary to whisper yet, but all their noises felt amplified in the empty hall.

Becca seemed to have the same sense. She didn't say anything at all, just pointed toward the stacks of folding chairs in the back near the retractable wall of the sanctuary. Eitan laughed quietly. "That's actually genius, Becks. No one's going to look in the High Holiday overflow chairs." They hurried to the back of the sanctuary and squished themselves in between the racks of plastic chairs.

They were just in time. As soon as they had stopped shifting and shoving while the chairs creaked around them, the temple secretary came in to do her final sweep. She turned off the light, which made Becca gasp at the sudden darkness, but Naomi clapped a hand over her friend's mouth, and the secretary didn't hear her. They waited a few more minutes, just in case she came back, then crept as quietly as they could out of the stacks of chairs. Eitan clicked on his key-chain flashlight, and they made their way through the dark to one of the pews in the back.

They huddled together in the weak glow of Eitan's flashlight on the cushioned seat of the pew, using one another's shoulders to prop themselves up and Eitan's relatively clean extra sweatshirt as a blanket stretched out as far as it could over the three of them. Naomi, who was always cold, squished into the middle of the group, while Becca, who preferred not to cuddle if she could help it, curled up with her back pressed against Naomi's arm. Eitan, who didn't have siblings and therefore always wanted to cuddle, draped an arm over both of them, though Naomi thought that might have also been because he was nervous in the dark temple. She was. Her skin was prickling, not quite in the same crawling way that the demon-woman at the mini golf course had caused, but something was happening. She thought back to the whispering shadows at Beth Torah and what Rabbi Levinson had said about congregations of ghosts, and curled more tightly under Eitan's arm.

"Are you scared?" she whispered. Beside her, Becca had already begun to snore softly. The ability to fall asleep literally anywhere was one of Becca's best talents.

Eitan let out a gusty breath. "Yes," he whispered back. "Aren't you?"

"Terrified," Naomi admitted. "We'll be okay, right?"

"Sure we will." Eitan sounded confident, but Naomi had a feeling it was a good thing she couldn't see his face in the dark. She scooted a little closer to Becca, pulling Eitan along with her, and tried to sleep.

Naomi woke up a few hours later to Becca's sharp elbow in her side. The feeling of static charge in the air was a lot stronger. Becca was sitting up, her breathing fast and nervous.

"Becks?" Naomi whispered.

Becca shushed her, then pointed over the top of the pew. Naomi peered into the dark where Becca was pointing and smothered a gasp. There were shapes moving in the gloom. They glowed slightly and didn't seem to touch the ground. As Naomi watched, the shapes solidified into people, and the darkness of the sanctuary lifted to something more like twilight. There were dozens of them, packed into the pews. More than Naomi had ever seen on a regular Shabbat morning. If they had been solid, Naomi thought, they probably would have had to pull back the partition wall to fit everyone. As it was, the people didn't seem to mind occasionally overlapping with a neighbor in a way that wouldn't have been possible if their bodies had been fully corporeal. Naomi thought she saw a man's elbow pass completely through the stomach of the woman next to him. They settled into the pews, chatting among themselves like it really was a normal Shabbat service. It didn't look like they had spotted Naomi and her friends in the back. Naomi tugged Becca down beside her.

"You can see them?" she whispered. Becca nodded. Naomi swallowed. "What do you think it is?" It was a stupid question. She knew what this was just as sure as she had known what the flickering shadows in her own synagogue were. Still.

Becca shook her head. "I don't know. They don't really look . . . solid. Nae, could there actually be ghosts?" She reached over Naomi and pinched Eitan. He woke with a start and glared, but the two of them gestured to him to be quiet, and then, like Becca had before, Naomi pointed to the crowd of people beginning to pray. Eitan's eyes grew wide, but before he could say anything, someone tapped Naomi on the shoulder. She shivered.

"Excuse me, young lady, are you saving these seats for someone?" Naomi turned and met the eyes of a wizened old lady. She looked like any of the old ladies Naomi saw at temple, except she stepped right through the bench as she talked. Naomi shook her head. The woman smiled at her, absently shifting her handbag and voluminous floral skirt to sit down. Then she froze. "Oh dear. Oh my goodness. You're real children! You aren't dead at all! Oh my! Sylvia!" She waved frantically at another little old lady, who was making her slow way down the aisle. "Sylvia, these children are alive!"

The whole congregation turned to stare at them. Naomi could hear them muttering to one another. Then, as one, all the ghosts started to walk toward them. Eitan stood up on the bench, pulling Becca and Naomi with him. They huddled close as the ghosts pressed in tighter and tighter around them, muttering and staring and reaching out to touch until a voice from the front, low and commanding, said, "Enough."

The ghosts fell back, parting ways as an old man in a shining tallit stepped up and extended a hand toward Naomi and her friends. "I'm sorry, children. It has been a long time since we were joined by anyone living." He smiled wryly. "They get excited." He pulled his hand back when none of them took it and nodded, understanding. "I am Rabbi Gershon. Will you pray with us?"

"Do we have a choice?" Becca whispered.

"Of course you have a choice," the rabbi's ghost told them. "But we would be overjoyed if you would stay. You don't need to be afraid."

"We don't have anywhere else to go," Eitan pointed out. He didn't bother to whisper, since it seemed the ghosts could hear them either way.

Naomi nodded. "We'll stay."

The rabbi smiled. "Wonderful. We return to page three hundred and sixty-five," he called out to the congregation as he strode back to the podium.

With much muttering and sideways glances, and more than one ghost lingering a little too close for comfort until another ghost pushed them along, the congregation retreated to their pews and began to pray.

12

DEAD RABBIS STILL TELL STORIES

The service seemed to stretch forever, but also go by fast enough that Naomi had a hard time keeping up—"so like a normal service," Becca whispered—but the night was still dark and chilly when it ended. Slowly, the congregants faded away again until only the rabbi remained. He made his quiet, drifting way to where they still sat huddled in the back.

He settled in, leaning back on the bench in front of them so that he could see them all. "Now," he said, "why don't you tell me your story?"

The three of them shared a look that Naomi

decided to interpret as meaning, *Why not? This is hardly the weirdest thing to happen to us this week.*

"Okay," Naomi said. "Here's how it started."

Rabbi Gershon listened to their story as attentively as Rabbi Levinson had—maybe more so, since he knew their story was real—occasionally stroking his beard and making *hmm* noises like Naomi's grandpa did when he was trying to show he was listening. Except for the slight strangeness of being dead, Rabbi Gershon was a comforting figure. Naomi couldn't help thinking that Rabbi Levinson was all well and good, but Rabbi Gershon, with his wise old eyes and his beard, was how rabbis were meant to be. Deena and her friends would *never* have crushes on Rabbi Gershon.

"Well," he said when they were finally done, "it *is* an adventure you're embarking on, isn't it? Very brave children, to approach a Golem on your own." He chuckled. "Though I suppose to you *we're* likely the more frightening prospect."

"No," Naomi said quickly. "Not at all. We"—she waved her hand a little aimlessly—"we're just feeling a bit overwhelmed."

"And understandably so. It's not every day we meet people who are able to see us, let alone children. You *have* been having an adventure," he repeated. He *hmm*ed and stroked his beard again. "Now, then, you have a Bat Mitzvah coming up, yes? And you, son, a Bar Mitzvah as well?"

Becca raised her hand. "And me too."

"January babies," they chorused automatically, and it was such a normal moment in the completely abnormal situation they had found themselves in that Naomi felt the urge to giggle.

Rabbi Gershon smiled. "Well, then, does anyone have the Parashat Shemot?" They looked at him blankly, and he laughed again. "Ah. I see. All right, who gets the burning bush bit?"

"Oh!" Naomi raised her hand. "That's me!"

"Very nice. An excellent passage, that one. And fitting. Can you tell me why?"

"Don't we get enough Bat Mitzvah prep from the living?" Becca muttered. Naomi felt Eitan shove at her behind her back.

"Well," Naomi said slowly, "the rabbi says it's about responsibility, and Cantor Debbie says that in that passage we focus on the word 'hineni.'"

"Excellent. And why is that?" Rabbi Gershon's

eyes were sparkling, and the strange translucence of him made it an odd thing, like Naomi was looking at stars through a veil.

"When Moses says 'hineni,' he is saying that he is present before God and committed to listening and taking on the duties that he is asked to," Naomi recited, as she had recited a million times before with Cantor Debbie on her tape.

The rabbi tapped one ghostly finger to his nose, and Naomi was a little surprised it didn't pass right through. "Like Moses before us, we have a responsibility," he said, "to be present when we are called to righteous work." He leaned toward them, and Naomi couldn't suppress a shudder at the way the air got colder. Eitan's fingers found her elbow and gripped tightly. "What do you think of that?" Rabbi Gershon asked.

Naomi let out a frustrated huff. She was exhausted, she was dirty, and she was scared. She had spent the last two weeks responsible for a Golem she had never asked for, being followed by magic she hadn't even known existed, and the last thirty-six hours diving headfirst into the supernatural with no weapons except Becca's maps and Rabbi Levinson's book of stories.

"I think that I'm not even turning thirteen for another week and I'm trying as hard as I can to be good, and it's not enough. It's never enough! It's not fair! I don't want to be responsible for the world. I'm still learning how to be responsible for myself!"

"Hmm. A troubling thought, it's true." The rabbi nodded. "We do everything in our power to bring about change. We choose the righteous path when we can, we take responsibility when we must, and still it feels like drops of water in a pond. A troubling thought," he repeated. "Who are we that God should demand such works from us? Then again, who was Moses?" He pointed at the three of them. "Did Moses save the entire world, or did he save his corner of it? When we have a Passover seder, do we celebrate what he accomplished or curse him for not freeing slaves across the globe?" He didn't seem to need an answer from them, though he smiled a bit at their wide-eyed looks.

"There is a saying that you are not obligated to complete the work, but neither are you free to abandon it." Rabbi Gershon stroked his beard and sat back. "You, my friends, seem to be very intent on not abandoning your work, so I will say this. The first part of that saying is just as important, if not more so, for living a righteous life without becoming discouraged. In these difficult times, you must remember that *you are not obligated to complete the work*. Every day, we do what we can, but you are not responsible for all the world's ills. You can't fix everything, children, and in trying, you will only cause yourselves pain."

There was a whisper in the air around them, and Sylvia appeared in the pew next to Becca, who squeaked and pressed herself closer to Naomi. "He's right, you know," the old lady said. "Rabbi Gershon is the wisest rabbi we've had here in centuries." She held out a tray that hadn't been there a moment before. It looked very normal. Shiny and plastic, with the sort of paisley pattern favored by grandmas everywhere. "Cookie?"

"Ah." The rabbi intercepted Eitan's hand as he reached for the plate. "Better not." He clicked his tongue chidingly at Sylvia. "None of those tricks. You know better."

Sylvia pouted. "They're such charming children," she said.

"And they will be charming *adults* in their time. We aren't demons, Sylvia; we don't trap people here."

Sylvia *hmmph*ed, and disappeared with her cookies as suddenly as she had come. Eitan retracted his hand slowly, looking pale, though Naomi wasn't sure if that was because of the near miss with Sylvia's cookie trap or because Rabbi Gershon had touched him. The rabbi shook his head, like Sylvia had made a slightly off-color joke rather than apparently trying to trap them in the weird, ghostly twilight world they had found themselves in. "She misses her grandchildren, I think," he told them kindly.

None of them had an answer for that. Though a different thought was bugging Naomi. "Fine," she said, "so we need to cut ourselves some slack. But I *am* responsible for this Golem. And what about Golems, anyway? They're obligated to complete any 'work' they're given. They're not free to abandon anything." She could feel something curling in her stomach that felt a lot like guilt, and she suddenly missed the small, funny creature that fit into her American Girl doll sweaters and sat beside her on her bed when he wasn't busy completing tasks she had given him.

Rabbi Gershon sighed. "A Golem's obligation is why they become so dangerous, in the end. When we don't have the ability to step back, when the work becomes the only thing in our minds, absent any moments of rest, gratitude, or pleasure, we lose sight of the reasons the work is important. Golems are made to work, but there is no love driving them. Work is only fulfilling when one chooses to engage in it; otherwise, it is servitude. No being can survive in a condition of constant servitude, and so the Golem does the only thing it can: it works, until the work itself becomes a source of destruction, and the Golem is able to find rest."

Naomi scrubbed a shaky hand across her eyes, wondering when she had started crying. "What if we didn't mean for that to happen?" she whispered. "What if we love it?"

The ghostly rabbi inclined his head a little. "That," he said in his wise, comforting voice, "would be a beautiful thing." He reached out and patted each of their heads in turn. It felt like being swatted very gently with an ice pack. "And now I think it's time you rested. You have a difficult road ahead of you, and you will need your strength." He guided them to lie back down in the pew and draped Eitan's sweatshirt over them. "Sleep, children. We will watch over you. You will be safe."

When they woke in the morning, Rabbi Gershon was gone, along with the rest of the ghosts. It was early enough, though, that the actual synagogue staff hadn't arrived yet. Naomi got the feeling that someone had woken them, and she sent out a silent thank-you to the ghostly rabbi for looking out for them. They found apple juice, broccoli, carrot sticks, and string cheese in the kitchen for breakfast—snacks for the kindergarteners, most likely—and packed some extra portions for the road. They all used the bathroom and did the best they could to make it look like they hadn't biked for several hours the day before and then slept in a temple pew. It felt like a bit of a lost cause; Naomi thought she would need to shower for at least an hour to get all the dust and sweat from the day before off her. She stuck her head under the sink and got her hair wet enough that her curls defrizzed a bit, at least. Then the three of them slipped out of the synagogue into the blue light of the early morning.

Becca led the way back to the main road, consulting her maps on the best route for them to continue northward. Naomi looked out at the Golem's trail stretching away along the dusty road. It went as far as she could see, and she didn't think she was imagining the glimpses of gold flashing in the distant foothills. "I think we're going to need some better wheels," she admitted. "Becks, any bus lines through here?"

Becca shook her head. "Not unless we go really out of our way."

Eitan groaned. "Well, at least when we go back to school, we won't have to lie to Ms. Brauer about whether we exercised over the break."

Naomi laughed. "Thanks for giving us a bright side, Eitan. All right, then, bikes it is."

They rode for close to half an hour before Becca insisted they break for snacks. Naomi agreed; it wasn't hot, but the sun was bright and glaring above them, and her skin felt itchy from the dust and sweat. They stopped their bikes, and Naomi pulled out a container that she had filled with vegetables from the synagogue's kitchen. She was busy passing out carrots when she looked up and saw the bus.

"Becks," she said, "I thought you said there weren't any buses that came through here."

"There aren't," Becca said without looking up.

"So what's that?"

Becca and Eitan both turned to look where Naomi was pointing. Sure enough, there was a city bus coming up the long stretch of road toward them. Naomi turned quickly to her other side. "There!" A bus stop. One of the shiny new ones the city had put up in their neighborhood in the last few years. It was so close that she was shocked they hadn't seen it before. She grabbed the container of vegetables back from Eitan and shoved it in her bag. "Let's go!"

They made it just in time, panting and red-faced from the unexpected sprint on their bikes. Naomi was even itchier from the sweat and dust after rushing like that, the feeling prickling like ants crawling up her arms. Something in her mind suggested that wasn't a totally normal feeling, but it was a slippery thought to hold on to. Mostly, Naomi couldn't wait to get into the air-conditioning of the bus. The bus pulled up to the stop just as they reached it, and the driver opened the door. "Hello there!" He was a kindly looking old man, balding and round, and grinning at the three of them like they were the most exciting people he had ever met. "This your bus?"

"Um," Naomi said, unsure if it was a bus that they wanted or not.

"We're trying to get northeast, going up to the recreation areas," Becca told him, talking over her. "Are you going that direction?"

The bus driver laughed. "Am I going that direction? Sure I am! I'm going straight up northeast to the recreation areas, if you'd believe it!" He was so cheerful that Naomi found herself smiling. Eitan, too, was grinning at the driver. Even Becca, who never smiled at strangers, wasn't scowling.

"Great!" Naomi said. She pulled out her TAP card, then faltered when she realized there wasn't a scanner. She looked back at the bus driver. "Are these okay, or do we need bus tokens or something?" She was pretty sure no one used bus tokens anymore, but they didn't ride public transit outside of their own neighborhood very often, and Naomi wasn't sure if the protocol for these sorts of things changed from place to place. The driver just laughed again.

"Don't you worry about a thing. Just hop on. There's a bike rack in the back."

"That's great," Naomi said again. She felt less worried than she had in days. The bus driver was going to get them exactly where they needed to be.

13

EITAN FINDS
AN EXORCISM ON
THE INTERNET

They settled into seats at the back of the bus.
There was no one else there, which was lucky. It
meant there was plenty of room on the bike rack,
and the three of them could stretch out their tired
legs in their own seats. Becca was squirming, still
trying to get comfortable as the bus started moving. She was pulling at her sweatshirt and scowling. That was just how Becca got sometimes,
though. Usually, Naomi tried to help her figure
out what was bothering her, but she couldn't
muster up the worry. Naomi scratched absently

at her own arms, still feeling the crawling-ant-itchiness. Eitan, on her other side, was rubbing at the back of his neck like there was a mosquito. She smiled at him. Itchy as she was, the bus was so comfortable, and she was so tired. She thought about taking a nap in the cool, dust-free space.

"Do you kids like riddles?" The bus driver's sudden question startled Naomi out of her daze.

Eitan, looking equally startled, said, "What?"

"Riddles," the bus driver repeated. He turned his head to look at them, smiling, and Becca grabbed Naomi's arm as the bus swerved across the lanes of traffic, but none of the other cars on the road seemed to notice. Naomi patted Becca's hand absently. The comfortable doziness of the moment had been interrupted, but the bus was still cool and pleasant, and the bus driver seemed like he knew what he was doing. She trusted him not to crash.

Becca's hand tightened on Naomi's arm. The driver didn't turn back to the wheel. His eyes stayed fixed on the kids. "How many bagels can you eat on an empty stomach?" Naomi stared at him. Beside her, Becca and Eitan seemed just as confused. "Go on," the driver said. "How many?"

"Don't you think you should look at the road?" Becca asked nervously. Some of the fog in Naomi's brain started to clear in the face of Becca's nerves. Her skin was *crawling*.

"The road is fine. It's there. The road is always there, and I am always on the road." The driver smiled wider, and it was strange. Naomi felt like she shouldn't have been able to see that many of his teeth. "Answer the riddle. It's an easy one. How many bagels?"

"Four," Eitan said, picking a number at random.

The bus driver clucked. "Oh dear. Not a good start. The answer is one. Once you eat one bagel, your stomach isn't empty anymore!" The bus driver's smile got even wider. The bus skidded back across the lanes and rumbled along the shoulder. Becca screamed. That was not the right move, Naomi realized, as the bus driver frowned. Something was *wrong*. "Oh dear," he said again. "Let me straighten out." He turned his body more fully to the front of the bus and took hold of the steering wheel again. His head did not turn with him. Naomi's stomach clenched. Eitan gasped harshly, even as he clapped a hand over

Becca's mouth before she could scream again, and tugged her sideways. Her hold on Naomi's arm meant they both went tumbling into Eitan's row of seats. The three of them held on to one another tightly. The pleasant fog in Naomi's mind was gone, and the warning voices in her head were *screaming*. She put a finger to her lips. "Play along," she whispered urgently. "We have to figure out how to get off the bus." Becca and Eitan nodded. Becca's lips were white with how hard she was trying to keep quiet. The three of them sat up and peered over the seat.

"Let's try another one," the driver said. His voice was getting louder. "Who knows what other people are missing?" He gave the steering wheel a giant heave, and the bus turned down a side road Naomi hadn't noticed was there. There were no cars.

"Um." Eitan's face was screwed up in thought. "A psychic?"

"Wrong!" the driver bellowed. He stood up and walked toward them. The bus kept moving. "I'll give you one more try. You seem like clever children. Guess again!"

"A thief!" Becca yelled. Her eyes were squeezed

tightly shut, and her grip on Naomi's arm was cutting off her circulation. "It's a thief. He knows what people are missing because he has it."

The driver stopped advancing. "Very good. Very good. Very clever. I've missed clever brains like yours. Another!" He scrambled into the seat in front of them and peered over the back of it. "A man is dreaming of a journey at sea with his mother and father. The ship starts to sink! He can save only one person, but he wants to save both. What should he do?"

Naomi stared at him. His eyes were wide and black and empty. His smile was back, and even bigger. Naomi could almost count all thirty-two teeth in his mouth. He swayed with the movement of the bus still trundling along the dirt road with no one at the wheel and waited. "What are you?" she asked him.

He laughed. It wasn't a nice sound. "I am a man," he said. "A poor man, down on his luck." He pulled a ridiculously tragic face. "A wanderer. A lost soul. A victim of demons and curses, and men's cruelty." He bared his teeth again, though this time it wasn't a smile. "Don't you know the stories, kid?"

This time Eitan knew the answer. "A dybbuk," he breathed. Naomi and Becca both turned sharply to look at him.

"How do you know that?" Becca hissed.

"I've been doing research!" Eitan said. "It's in the stories Rabbi Levinson gave us. Evil spirits possessing people."

The dybbuk laughed. "A better answer than the last. Correct, though my circumstances are unusual. Tell me, will you help me? Or will you abandon me and leave me bound to my curse like you left the poor Golem? Bound and abandoned and set loose on the world." He pulled another horrible face. "What will the man do? His poor parents, shipwrecked at sea!"

"We didn't abandon the Golem," Naomi said. "We're going to get him."

"Going. Gone. Went. Done. You bound him to his task, young lady; can you cut the ropes? What does the sinking man do?"

"Just let us go!" Becca's spine was rigid. Naomi could feel her friend's fear turning into anger. "We don't know how to break your curse, and honestly, I think someone probably cursed you for a reason."

The dybbuk laughed again. "Oh, probably, probably. I wasn't a very nice man in my life, it's true. My luck ran out and I died, but I stayed here with my unfinished business, and that suited me just fine. Then I crossed the wrong demon, and he bound me to this stretch of road. No more new bodies. Stuck in my last shape, with that shape's horrible old job with no one to take me new places. I have been *so* bored." He grinned. "But now *you're* here. Some clever children, mixed up in magic, waiting for a bus. I was *delighted* to find you on my route. Not many can see me. My lucky day. What does the drowning man do?"

The bus swerved hard and hit a pothole, throwing them all against one another. "We don't want to play!" Becca shouted.

"Who's playing?" The dybbuk snarled. The bus lurched the other way, coming up onto two tires. "No more driving for me, I think. You're on my bus. You're bound to my rules. Who is the cleverest? That is the one I will take. I haven't been a child in a long time. What does the dreaming, drowning, desperate man do?"

Eitan pulled his phone from his pocket, keeping it low. "Stall him," he whispered.

Becca and Naomi gave him matching incredulous looks. "Stall him?" Becca whispered back.
"Are you completely insane, you—"

"Becca!" Naomi said loudly. "Becca, you have
a riddle, right?" She looked at the dybbuk. "It's
our turn, isn't it? You've already asked two. We
should get to ask one."

This seemed to please the dybbuk. "Oh, very
good. An equal game. That's just fine. Never let
it be said that I'm not a fair man. If I were still a
man, of course." He winked one empty eye like
they were sharing a secret.

"Go on, Becks," Naomi said weakly. The look
Becca gave her would have made her hide behind
Eitan on a normal day, but this day had become
decidedly not normal.

Becca took a deep, shaking breath. "Um," she
said. "Uh. What gets wet as it dries?"

Naomi nodded rapidly. That was a good one. It
had been on one of their Popsicle sticks last week
and had made Deena roll her eyes and kick them
out of her room. Eitan was speed-reading next
to her, muttering under his breath. The dybbuk
looked even less pleased than Deena had. "Too
easy," he complained. "Disappointingly simple."

"Sorry we don't spend all our time thinking up riddles," Becca growled. "*We* still have lives."

The dybbuk cackled. "It's true, and soon I will have one of them. Will the rest of you still be friends with me, children, if I take one of your bodies?" He leaned forward hungrily. "A towel gets wet as it dries, wicked child. Now. Again. A man is dreaming of a journey at sea with his mother and father. The ship starts to sink! He can save only one person, but he wants to save both, what should he do?"

Eitan plunged his hand into Naomi's backpack, pulled out the plastic container of vegetables, and yanked open a corner of the lid. "He should wake up," he said. He read out a string of what sounded like Hebrew off his phone, but Naomi had never heard any of the words before. The dybbuk screamed. The bus shuddered. Then it steadied, and the dybbuk dropped back, his eyes wide. He wasn't smiling at all anymore. "You don't have the power to do that," he sneered. "Look at you, a clever child—but just a child. You're no rabbi to say those words."

Eitan scowled and read the words again, changing his pronunciation. The dybbuk screamed again; the bus shook so hard Naomi's teeth clacked together painfully, then settled again. Eitan growled in frustration. The dybbuk was breathing hard, like he was recovering from a shock. He was beginning to look worried. "What's wrong?" Naomi whispered.

"Stupid variable Hebrew pronunciation," Eitan muttered. "Say that word." He pointed to a bit of text. It wasn't written in Hebrew letters, thank goodness, just a transliteration. Naomi read it aloud, sounding it out slowly. Eitan nodded. "Yeah, that's probably it. Thanks." He took a big breath and read the whole text again, emphasizing the word Naomi had read for him. The dybbuk let out a sound that wasn't human enough to call a scream, and then Naomi was hitting the ground at a roll. She screamed almost as loud as the dybbuk, bringing her arms up to protect her head. She rolled to a stop in the dirt, then felt the air leave her lungs all over again as Becca crashed into her.

The lump that was Becca said, "Ow."

"Yeah," Naomi agreed hoarsely. "Where's Eitan?"

"Here." He was crouched in the dirt a little

ways away, clutching the plastic container to his chest. Their bikes lay in a heap next to him. There was no sign of the dybbuk or the bus. They were alone on the road.

"What did you do?" Becca demanded. The back of her sweatshirt was torn, and her hair had completely escaped from her braid and was matted with dirt.

"Honestly?" Eitan said. "I'm not sure. I googled exorcisms, and found one with a transliteration for the Hebrew." His nose was bleeding a bit, and he wiped it on his sleeve, wincing. "It feels like my brain got put through a blender, but"—he held up the Tupperware—"I think it worked."

Naomi let out a breath. "It worked," she confirmed. "Can't you feel it?" The pins and needles were gone. Her skin felt raw all over but *clean*. Well. Relatively. She leaned forward and prodded at the Tupperware. "It's *in* there?"

Eitan scratched at his neck, frowning. "Yeah, I feel it," he said, rubbing at the back of his neck again with his free hand. He shook the Tupperware. "I *think* it's in there. The whole thing got really hot for a second and glowed red, and then we ended up out here."

Becca laughed. It was only a little shaky. "Well, I'm not eating those vegetables now."

"No," Naomi agreed.

Eitan nodded his agreement. His usually warm, tanned skin was gray and pale, and there was a scrape on his cheek. When he ran a nervous hand over his head, dust floated up out of his short-cropped hair. Naomi took a moment to be grateful that the cool weather meant they were all wearing long sleeves and jeans. Things could have looked a whole lot worse for them.

Behind Naomi, Becca said, "Bury it." Naomi jumped. She hadn't realized Becca had gotten so close.

"The Tupperware?" she asked.

Becca nodded. "We're not carrying it with us. And if we leave it here, it'll get opened one way or another. We have to bury it so that thing can't get out again."

Neither Naomi nor Eitan was going to argue with that. None of them wanted to face anything like the dybbuk ever again. They spent a few minutes chipping away at the dry earth with the back end of Naomi's flashlight and a metal spoon that Becca found in her bag. Then they gave up and just dug in the dirt with their hands. They were already so dirty, all their attempts at pulling themselves together at the temple ruined by their tumble onto the road. A little more dirt didn't matter. They managed to create a shallow hole, and Eitan stuck the Tupperware in the bottom. Then they swept the loose dirt back over it and stood around it for a minute, catching their breath.

"If anyone wants to go home, speak up now," Naomi said. "This is more than we bargained for, and I think things are going to keep getting weirder. This doesn't have to be your problem."

In answer, Becca shot her a scornful look and punched her in the shoulder while Eitan turned away and started pulling at the bikes. "Can you still see where we need to go?" he asked Naomi.

She nodded. The Golem's path was clear enough. They had been taken off course by the dybbuk and his bus, but Naomi could still see the glowing footprints striking out north and east toward where the buildings became fewer and farther between and eventually gave way to wilderness.

"Then let's go," Becca said, trying to coax her hair back into something close to a braid.

Naomi nodded again, feeling a little like she might cry if she tried to talk. Becca tied off her hair and, in silence, the three of them buckled their helmets back on, turned toward the path left by their missing Golem, and started to ride.

14

THERE'S ALWAYS A CHABAD

They didn't make it far. They had left the temple in the morning, but they had lost more time than Naomi had realized while trapped on the bus with the dybbuk. It was already starting to get dark. The suburbs of Santa Clarita were relatively remote compared to where they had stopped at the synagogue, but it was still evening in the city, and there was magic in the air around them.

Naomi pulled her bike to a stop, and her friends did the same, braking when they came level with her. "We need to stop soon," Naomi said. "If we try to keep moving, we're going to get hit by a car or caught by another demon."

"Definitely. Okay, whose house tonight?" Becca asked, already starting a text to her mom.

"Mine," Eitan decided. "And I'll tell my parents I'm at Troy's. That way they won't call your parents. Troy will cover for me, and my mom hates his mom, so she won't call her to check if I'm there in case Mrs. Lewis wants to chat with her."

Becca and Naomi agreed and sent out the messages. Then there was the much more important question of where they were actually going to sleep that night. Becca hummed thoughtfully as she examined her maps. "There are a few hotels nearby. How much money do we have between us?"

Naomi and Eitan looked at each other. Naomi shrugged. "Seventy-six dollars. Forty from the piggy bank fund, plus Eitan's Bar Mitzvah money."

Eitan made a face at her. "And I have the ten dollars Mom gave me for snacks and my dad's emergency credit card, but if I use that he'll know I'm not at Troy's."

Becca nodded. "And I have twenty-three dollars and thirty-seven cents left from my babysitting money." She grimaced. "And none of us is eighteen, so we probably can't stay in a hotel any-way." She prodded at the map, her tongue stick-ing out the side of her mouth in concentration. The bit of her braid that Naomi could see below her helmet was even more of a tangled mess than it had been when they set out, although Becca had rebraided it twice. The knees of her jeans were caked with ground-in dirt from where she had hit the road after the dybbuk's bus disap-peared. There were probably bruises underneath that dirty denim. "Aha!" she cried.

"What?" Naomi and Eitan demanded together. Becca's face was smug, like she had just found a mint-condition map at a garage sale for a dollar.

"I *told* you it was a good cover story."

"What was?" Eitan said, exhaustion and frus-tration making his voice sharp.

"A Chabad," Becca said, jabbing her finger at the small map on her phone so the description of the location popped up on the screen. Naomi leaned in. Sure enough, the small bubble on the map read *Chabad of Santa Clarita Valley: A cen-ter for traditional Judaism serving the commu-nity of Santa Clarita Valley.* Becca smirked up at them and said again, "I *told* you."

The Chabad was surprisingly close. After only another half an hour of riding—the sun now well and truly below the horizon—the three of them stood blinking in the harsh lights of a tiny strip mall. Naomi looked at the small blue sign in front of her, wondering if she was hallucinating.

"I can't believe there is *actually* a Chabad in Santa Clarita," Eitan said.

"Never doubt my geography," Becca said.

"I did doubt you, but I never will again. It's really there," Naomi said. Though she knew that Becca's aunt Ruth lived in Calabasas and would almost definitely *not* be there, no matter what Becca had told Jonah the day before.

"Well, your aunt Ruth definitely isn't there with dinner," Eitan grumbled, echoing Naomi's thoughts. "And I never doubted your geography, just your sanity. I can't believe Jonah believed you." Eitan's grumpiness did nothing to make Becca less smug, and even he had to admit it was a lucky find. The Chabad was sandwiched between a medical supply store and a dance studio, and they would have missed it without Becca's keen sense of direction. It was possibly the smallest Chabad Naomi had ever seen. She wasn't sure how they did any kind of services, let alone run preschool or community events in that tiny space.

However small it was, though, it was also the most reassuring thing Naomi had encountered all week. Here, huddled together under the weird yellow glow of the streetlamps in unfamiliar territory without any adults they knew, the danger of what they were doing felt more real. In the dark, the fear that had lingered since they had defeated the dybbuk returned, sharp and sour in the back of her throat. The familiar lettering on the sign for the Chabad gave her an anchor. She pulled on the door.

"It's locked," Becca said helpfully.

"Yes, I can see that." Naomi tugged on the handle again, her heart sinking. She didn't even know if they would have been able to spend the night, but the idea of just a few minutes sitting somewhere safe and familiar had been the only thing keeping her going over those last miles on their bikes. "What now?"

"Can you still see the trail?" Eitan asked. Naomi was really starting to hate that question. Eitan met the glare she turned on him with a fierce look of his own, and Naomi sighed. She looked at where the glowing footprints ran across the street, going farther north still through the neighborhoods that surrounded the strip mall.

"Yes, I can see it." There was something else, though, something that didn't feel like it would be friendly if it caught up with them. Naomi looked around. She couldn't see anything, but those same just-out-of-earshot chittering voices were starting up again, louder now that the wind blowing by while they rode was gone, and there was nothing to drown them out.

"Nae?" Becca asked. "You okay?"

"I'm not sure." She reached for her friends' hands. "Can you hear that?" After a moment, Becca and Eitan turned to her with wide eyes. Naomi swallowed. She had been hoping it was just nerves, or, failing that, that it was just her. She didn't like that Eitan and Becca could see and feel the magic now. It felt like a sign that things were going to keep getting worse.

"What is it *now*?" Eitan demanded. It wasn't quite a whine; his voice was too shaky for that.

"I don't know," Naomi said. "Was there anything else that could be useful on that site where you found the exorcism? Or in the book Rabbi Levinson gave us?" Eitan pulled the book out of his backpack. It was already full of bookmarks and notes. Naomi could see Eitan's scribbly handwriting on many of the colorful Post-it notes peeking through the pages. Eitan flipped through the book quickly, checking all his notes, then shook his head.

"Nothing about feeling magic as it gets closer, or how to tell what's coming. I think the rabbi was right that that doesn't show up in a lot of books. I get the feeling that not all ghosts are as friendly as Rabbi Gershon, though, and this feels mean. Did the other ones feel this mean? What about the lady at the golf course? You escaped her okay," Eitan said hopefully. Then he faltered. "Oh. But that creepy kid and that couple earlier didn't feel this bad."

Naomi grimaced. "Yeah."

"Well, that's terrifying," Becca said. "I vote we try to avoid whatever's making these voices."

Naomi swallowed. The noise was getting closer. "I don't think we're going to be able to. Not if we stick around here." She looked at her friends, then cast one last longing look at the locked door. "I think maybe we should get going."

They were about to step off the sidewalk back into the night when the door to the Chabad center swung open, and a young woman in a practical black skirt and a flour-dusted apron poked her head out. The three of them jumped so high, Naomi thought it was a miracle that none of them fell over or hit the low overhang of the strip mall. The woman looked at them curiously. "Are you guys okay?"

"Oh, yes," Naomi said, trying to steady her breathing. "We're just—"

"Waiting for our parents," Becca supplied. It would have been more believable if she wasn't white as a sheet and holding her maps out in front of her like a weapon. Or if they hadn't actually been hoping to stay the night at the Chabad. Naomi despaired of Becca's terrible cover stories.

"Yeah," Eitan added, reaching out to push the tube of maps in Becca's hands down and shooting her an irritated look. "They're just . . . running late."

The woman didn't seem convinced. "It's pretty late already." When that didn't pull any more information from the three of them besides a shrug from Naomi and a few strange faces that might have been an attempt to look innocent from Becca, the woman sighed. "Well, why don't you wait inside? I'm making a bunch of challah dough for the preschoolers to shape tomorrow. I'll be here a while yet."

Naomi nodded quickly. Getting in was the most important part; if they had to, they could come up with a reason to stay later. As soon as the door closed behind them, the whispering voices that had been growing in the darkness of the empty parking lot quieted, and the sense of magic in the air faded away. Eitan let out a breath of relief that Naomi agreed with wholeheartedly. None of them had liked the idea of riding off into the night with whatever it was that was causing that noise following close behind.

The Chabad was small—smaller than any temple Naomi had ever been in—with a wide-open room with industrial carpeting and folding chairs and tables stacked along the walls. It looked like it served as both sanctuary and community room. There were a few doors off the side that were closed, though one had a bathroom sign and another a bright, finger-painted poster that said

PRESCHOOL. The kitchen was off to the right of the big room.

The woman who had brought them inside introduced herself as Masha and set them to kneading challah dough after supervising them through the most thorough hand-washing Naomi had ever done in her life. Masha was the Chabad rabbi's oldest daughter, it turned out, and was in charge of the preschool class. She worked the dough twice as quickly as they did and had no problem carrying on a conversation with three strange children who had appeared on her door-step at night. She seemed pleased to find out they were Jewish and asked them rapid-fire questions about their Jewish education as she worked, which they answered as best they could. They helped her make and knead dough for more than an hour, then helped her clean the kitchen space. By the time they were finished, it was nearly mid-night, and their excuse that their parents were on the way was running thin.

Masha looked at them closely, and Naomi wondered if she looked as pale and ragged as she felt. Eitan and Becca were certainly looking worse for wear. She hoped maybe they seemed less like they'd been fighting off dybbuks and sleeping in temples and more like they had just had a big day of dirt biking, or something. They stood there silently, submitting to Masha's long inspection until she seemed to come to some sort of conclusion. "You never called your parents," she said. It wasn't a question. They shook their heads. "Are you going to?" They shook their heads again, and Masha frowned, though she didn't seem that surprised. "And I'm guessing you won't let me call them either, hmm?" Another shake. Masha sighed. "Well, it's not like I can force their phone numbers out of you. Can you tell me if this is a situation where I need to call the police?" she asked them.

"It's not," Naomi said quickly. "We're not runaways, and we're not missing. We just . . . we're looking for something, and we need to keep going."

"We're geocaching!" Eitan said in a fit of inspiration.

"Geocaching," Masha said. Her face was even more skeptical than Naomi's mom's when Naomi told a particularly bold lie about whether or not she had done her chores. "And what's that?"

"You know," Becca said. "Someone buries

something somewhere and leaves coordinates, and then we have to track it down."

"Yeah," Naomi echoed, though she had never heard of geocaching before. "And if we go home we'll have to start all over, and we've, um, just ridden really far already."

"All right." Masha nodded, but she looked less like she believed their story and more like she was choosing not to question it. "Let's call it a compromise. I won't call the police, but I'm also not going to let you ride off on your bikes into the mountains in the middle of the night. Let me take you to my parents. They live right over there." She gestured vaguely toward one of the neighborhoods across the street. "You can sleep in the living room on the couches, and they'll feed you breakfast in the morning, and then you can go back to . . . geocaching."

Naomi grinned. Her mom always said never to go anywhere with strangers, but her *mama* had always said that if Naomi were lost anywhere in the world, the first thing she should look for was a Chabad house, and they would help her. Naomi was feeling pretty lost, and her mama had never led her astray. Besides, Masha wasn't really a stranger anymore, anyway. Nobody could be a stranger after you helped them scrub flour out of the grout of a horrible, tiled countertop. "Okay," Naomi said. "Thank you. That's really nice of you. We'd love to stay over with your parents."

Masha shooed them outside while she locked up, then walked them and their bikes over to a nearby neighborhood, where she knocked softly on the door of a cheerful little house with a bright electric menorah in the window. A tired-looking woman in a light-blue head scarf answered the door. She watched them as Masha explained the situation, her hands propped on her wide hips and mouth pursed in a look that made Naomi feel like she was being sized up. "All right," Masha's mother finally said. "I'm Mrs. Greenberg." She eyed their messy hair and dirt-crusted sweat-shirts. "Do you kids have a change of clothes?" They shook their heads, and she pursed her lips at them again. "All right. You all need to shower, and you can borrow pajamas from the kids. I'll wash your clothes overnight." She nodded sharply at Masha, who disappeared down the hall and came back with a bundle of pajamas and a neat stack of linens. Her mother took them from her and waved at the three of them. "Go on, there's a bathroom on either side of the hall. Use the shampoo that's in there. Clean towels under the sink. Masha and I will get the couches set up while you bathe, and then maybe we all can get some sleep."

Naomi followed Becca and Eitan down the hall, splitting off to the bathroom on the right while Eitan turned left. She looked questioningly at Becca. "You want first?" Becca shook her head, and Naomi didn't need to be told twice. The shower was small, with bad water pressure, but it was the best thing that had happened to Naomi in days. She scrubbed at her hair until she thought it was in danger of falling out, then she got out and put on the clean pajamas. Becca knocked as Naomi was drying her hair, and she let her in and slipped into the hall. She waited until Becca cracked the door and threw her dirty clothes out, then she brought the laundry back down the hall to where Eitan was helping Mrs. Greenberg and Masha tuck sheets into the couches.

"Laundry room is past the kitchen," Mrs. Greenberg said. "Leave it there." Naomi did as she was told, dropping hers and Becca's clothes in a pile on top of Eitan's in the empty hamper. When she returned, the couches were ready, and Masha was gathering up her things. Naomi and Eitan waved as Masha kissed her mother goodbye and then offered them a smile.

"Thank you for your help with the challah. Good luck with your geocaching!" She winked. Naomi was sure Masha didn't believe their cover story, but it didn't really matter. They had a shower and a safe place to sleep. Naomi was calling this a win all around.

Then Becca came back from her shower, and Mrs. Greenberg got them settled in and shut off the lights. The darkness was soft, warm, and wonderfully silent. Naomi had thought she would be too wired from the day to sleep, but she was out before Mrs. Greenberg's footsteps stopped echoing in the hall.

In the morning, Naomi, Eitan, and Becca joined the five Greenberg children who still lived at home—"Masha and Yoni are both married now," a girl a couple of years older than them who introduced herself as Chava told them—and helped set out plates, forks, and juice while Mrs. Greenberg set out platters of scrambled eggs and fruit. The rabbi had had to go in early that morning, she told them, so they wouldn't meet him. Breakfast was different from the meals Naomi had at home. Louder, for one, but also more methodical. They all said the blessings together, which Naomi was happy to find she remembered, and then passed around the food in an order that was clearly an old routine. Mrs. Greenberg fed the baby, and Chava made sure two younger kids had food on their plates. Then she passed the food to Naomi and her friends and the second-oldest brother, who was thirteen and told them his name was Avi, and they were allowed to serve themselves. Then Chava took what was left. It was good, and the Greenbergs were welcoming, but Naomi could feel the Golem getting farther away with every minute they spent there. The good night's sleep and real food had taken the edge off some of the fear from the day before, and Naomi was eager to be on the road again.

Finally, after clean-up, dishes, and Mrs. Greenberg insisting on packing them a lunch, the three of them said their thank-yous and goodbyes and set out.

Becca was cranky. "I can't believe you guys

15

BECCA GETS
WHINY

The Golem's trail took them up toward the recreation areas near Castaic Lake, just like Becca
had told the dybbuk when they thought he was
a bus driver. They rode longer than any of them
had before, stopping for snacks and water every
few miles. Then, once when they reached the lake
and the campgrounds that surrounded it, Eitan
insisted they find a place to eat lunch. Naomi
agreed right away. She felt like her legs were
made of jelly. The three kids dragged themselves
to an empty picnic table and dropped onto the
bench with matching groans and a hiss of pain

when Eitan flexed his foot against a charley horse in his calf.

Becca flopped backward so she was stretched out completely on one of the picnic benches, her feet dangling to either side. "I don't know why," she said, "but I really didn't expect that tracking down a Golem was going to include so much biking. I think my legs are going to fall off."

Naomi had let her head fall to the questionably clean surface of the picnic table and wasn't particularly interested in sitting up again, but she reached out and patted blindly at whatever body part of Becca's was in reach, as a show of solidarity. She was pretty sure she got her elbow. Above them, Eitan grunted his agreement. "We should eat," he said.

"You always want to eat," Naomi retorted. But her stomach was clenched and hollow. The snacks they had stopped for had barely kept up with the number of calories they must be burning on their bikes. The big breakfast they had eaten with the Greenbergs seemed like a distant memory. Naomi's head felt like it weighed a hundred pounds, but she forced herself up and slowly pulled out the food they had left. The lunch Mrs. Greenberg had packed them would carry them through a few more hours, but there wasn't enough to save any for later, and the extra snacks they had taken from the temple were mostly depleted. She passed out the food, letting Eitan have the extra cookie. He took it from her with a grin.

"Cool. Do we have anything saved for the ride back?"

Naomi dug through the bag. "There's some cheese," she offered, "and a couple of granola bars."

"Dibs on the cheese," Becca said quickly.

Eitan grimaced. "All right, fine, I'll eat a granola bar. What have you got, Nae?" Naomi held up her own bar along with the juice box she had been saving since they left the temple the morning before.

"I have emergency candy and three boxes of raisins," Becca reported, her head buried in her backpack. "Oh! And some jerky! Enough for everyone to have a couple of pieces!"

Naomi wrinkled her nose; she hated jerky, especially the extra-spicy kind that Becca liked. Eitan patted her shoulder sympathetically. He hated jerky too. "We do what we have to, Nae.

You'll be eating your mama's horrible, gluten-free, vegan, not-even-really mac-'n-cheese before you know it."

"Bold words from the man whose mom sweeps his room for candy, Eitan."

"Totally fair," Eitan said, "but the point stands. Can you tell if we're getting close?"

They were. Naomi could see the trail getting clearer and brighter, like a beacon leading her on. Even so. "Not close enough," she said. "It's going to be a trek, and our bikes aren't really cut out for mountain trails."

"I bet we can make it," Becca said. "It's not like the trails are that bad." She poured the contents of a box of raisins into her hand, squeezed, and then put the entire sticky clump into her mouth. It was horrible, but also sort of fascinating to watch. Naomi leaned away as Becca, her mouth still full of half-chewed raisin glob, said, "We just have to hope there aren't any more dybbuks or ghosts in our way."

They set out about twenty minutes later, after they had rested for as long as they reasonably could. They tried to ride up the mountain, but Naomi had been right; their city bikes just weren't going to do the job. They made it only about a quarter of a mile to where the path curved away around a giant tree before the trail got too steep for bikes without good gears. When Eitan's bike hit a rock and wobbled so badly it almost knocked them all over like a row of dominoes, they agreed that they should double back and leave their bikes at the campground. Becca groaned as they turned once again to trudge back up the trail from the campground. "I can't believe we rode all this way and now we have to do it again on foot. Actually, just leave me here. For real. I can't walk anymore. My legs have never been this tired."

"None of us is happy about this, Becks, and *you're* the athlete," Eitan reminded her.

"So, I know what I'm talking about when I say this is just too much physical activity," she retorted. "Besides, I play softball. It's about the short sprint; it's not an endurance sport."

Naomi looked at Becca. She had dark circles under her eyes, and her hair beneath her bike helmet was sticking to her red, sweaty face in long dark strands. She was dirty, for all that Mrs. Greenberg had washed their clothes and replaced her torn sweatshirt with one of Masha's old ones. The day's riding had left them dusty and sore. She looked almost as miserable as Naomi felt, and Eitan didn't look much better, though his shorn hair kept him from looking *too* unkempt. "You can stay here," Naomi told them. "You don't have to come. I can go the rest of the way on my own."

Becca scowled. "Why do you keep trying to ditch us, Nae? Do you really think we're not going to be with you in this?"

"You were literally just saying—"

"I was *whining*," Becca cried. "If I'm not allowed to whine, this is going to get tragic really quickly. I'm obviously coming. *Jeez*." She rolled her eyes dramatically enough that she tripped on a stone and nearly fell over.

Eitan scoffed. "On second thought, maybe we should leave her. She's very clumsy." Becca lunged at Eitan and caught him in a headlock while he flailed and spluttered, and Naomi felt her doubt float away. They would finish this together.

She laughed a little at her friends' nonsense. "Okay, guys, let's save our energy for the hike."

Becca released Eitan with a smug look. "Well, what are we waiting for?"

. . .

They walked. They stopped to rest.

They walked. The trees all looked the same as they had earlier on the trail, down to the same broken branches and clusters of leaves.

They walked. The Golem's trail wavered and overlapped with itself in strange ways that Naomi had never seen before.

They walked. The hair on the back of Naomi's neck started to stand up, like there was a storm gathering around them, even though there wasn't a cloud in the sky. She could have sworn she had seen that weirdly shaped tree stump at least twice already, bent sideways and twisted like someone had put it through a taffy pull. Eitan was rubbing at his arms like there was itching powder in his sweatshirt. They kept walking.

"Something's wrong," Becca said. Naomi, out of breath and starting to shake with exhaustion, stumbled to a halt against a tree and turned to look at her friend.

"What do you mean?"

"Look at the sun," she said.

Eitan frowned. "Aren't we, like, explicitly not supposed to do that?"

"Oh my God, Eitan, be less of a know-it-all for thirty seconds and pay attention to what I'm saying." Becca held out her arms at an angle, squinting at the sky. "The angle of the sun is what it should be for early to midmorning, not afternoon. It's the same as it was when we were at the campsite, but we've been walking for hours. It should be all the way over there." She pointed.

"How do you know that?" Naomi asked. She pushed herself off the tree she was leaning against and sank down onto the weirdly shaped stump she kept seeing. The static in the air was getting worse. She could almost *smell* it, sharp and metallic and dangerous.

"Jonah gave me a solar map," Becca said, like that was a normal thing for Eitan's twenty-year-old cousin to have given her. "It's pretty cool, and it tells you how to map out your cardinal directions and figure out what time it is from the sun." She pointed again. "That sun is wrong."

Naomi rubbed her eyes. She was getting a headache. "How can the sun be wrong?"

"I don't know, but it is." Becca set her chin stubbornly. "I know how to read a map."

It was true; if Becca could do anything, it was

read a map. "So, what do we do?"

Becca frowned and pulled out her maps, shuffling until she got to the right one. She passed one end to Eitan for him to hold up so she could trace her finger along whatever trail she was following. She clicked her teeth and pulled out a second map of the recreation area. "These trails don't look right," she muttered. "Eitan." She held out the corner of another map, and he took it wordlessly. "Thanks." She bent over it.

Naomi was starting to shift a little restlessly when a voice behind them said, "You kids lost?" They looked up, immediately crowding together, Becca holding the plastic tube of her maps in front of her like it was her softball bat. It was a park ranger, a wiry woman in brown khaki, sensible boots, and a wide-brimmed hat covering close-cropped gray hair. They hadn't heard her walk up. She looked a little surprised to see them there at first, but then a slow smile spread across her weathered face. "Hello there, you three. Oh, you *are* lost."

Naomi squinted at her. Something buzzed up her spine like pent-up lightning, and she tasted pennies in the back of her throat. Goose bumps crawled along her skin. She edged closer to Eitan, eyeing the ranger warily. "Are you real?"

"Real?" The ranger looked perplexed, a crease forming between her thick, gray eyebrows. "Of course I'm real. Real as that tree you're sitting on." She gave them an encouraging smile. "Looks like you're trying to figure out some maps. Could I help?"

Becca clutched her maps to her chest, and Naomi took a half step in front of her automatically. Even if this woman had nothing to do with why the air felt like a thunderstorm, it wasn't okay to mess with Becca's maps. "No, thank you," she said. "But could you maybe point us toward the next trail marker? We're having trouble getting our bearings."

"Oh, sure thing, honey," the ranger said. "It's right up there." The ranger pointed. Her arm seemed very long. Naomi blinked a few times, sure she was seeing things, but the pointing arm kept stretching toward them, though the ranger never moved. The voices in Naomi's head *screamed*.

16

HOW FAR—
THAT FAR?

Naomi, Eitan, and Becca stood frozen for a moment, watching the ranger's arm come toward them, the pointing hand now a grasping claw that flexed in the air as it reached for them.

"You're kidding me," Eitan said. His words broke whatever strange compulsion was keeping them frozen. Eitan grabbed Naomi's hand, and they both stumbled backward into Becca, who gathered up her maps in one hand and the front of Naomi's sweatshirt in the other and started to run.

They ran in a stumbling huddle, trying to put

as much distance between themselves and the demon ranger as possible. Eventually, they came to a halt in a little clearing, and Naomi collapsed onto a tree stump, gasping for breath. Eitan dropped to the ground like a sack of potatoes, letting his head fall back into the dirt and leaves. Becca wrinkled her nose at him and leaned against a rock, pretending her hands weren't shaking as she tried to smooth out the creases that had formed in her maps while they ran.

"What was *that*?" Naomi gasped.

Eitan took a big gulping breath. "Some sort of demon, I think."

"Obviously. But what does it want with us?" Becca demanded.

Eitan shrugged a little, clearly not feeling as casual as he was trying to look now that the danger had passed. "What do any of the demons Naomi has run into want with us? I think they're just drawn to whatever magic stuck to us when we activated the Golem. From what Nae's said, I don't think people can usually see them. Maybe they're curious."

"*Curious*?" Becca demanded. "They keep trying to eat us or something!"

"They're demons, Becks. I don't know."

"Fine. How do we *stop* seeing them?"

"I don't know," Eitan said.

Naomi leaned toward them. "That was way more powerful than anything else we've run into so far. Couldn't you feel it?"

Becca scrubbed at her arms and nodded. "It felt like my skin was going to peel off."

"My mouth tasted like I was sucking on pennies," Eitan added. "Has that ever happened to you before, Nae?"

"No," Naomi admitted, "but it was definitely because of the demon. Like I said, I think it was super powerful."

Becca looked doubtful. "How did we get away if it was that powerful? Did we do something? Is it about distance?" She looked up at Eitan.

Eitan shrugged again, and Becca snarled, "What's the point of all your stupid research, then?" Naomi made a sympathetic face. Becca wasn't good at being sad or scared. She tended to snap at people so they didn't stick around long enough to see if she started crying, but Naomi could tell she was upset about her maps. She worked really hard to keep them in perfect condition.

Eitan scowled. Naomi held her breath. Eitan wasn't always as understanding about Becca's moods. He wasn't used to fighting with siblings like Naomi was. He didn't like getting yelled at, and he especially didn't like not always knowing why it happened. Sometimes it made him yell back instead of letting Becca calm down. He held his scowl for a moment longer. Then he sighed and looked away from Becca. Naomi relaxed. Even Eitan could tell it wasn't the time to pick a fight.

Eitan said, "I don't know. Everything I've read about demons is weird. They always seem to want to keep people in their world, but I don't really know why. As far as I can tell, they're just out to create mischief. We probably just got caught in a trap or something that the demon set to confuse people, and then when she figured out we could actually see her . . . well . . ."

"Well, are we un-caught now?" Becca demanded.

"No," Naomi said. She was looking at the stump she was sitting on. It was a weird shape, bent sideways and twisted like someone had put it through a taffy pull. She looked up at her friends. "I don't think we are."

"You kids lost?"

Becca let out a little shriek, and Eitan scrambled to his feet. There was a brief scuffle as all three of them tried to put the other two behind them, ending with them staring at the new arrival from a sort of lopsided triangular huddle. Naomi let out a breath of relief. It wasn't the same ranger. This was a much younger woman, her thick black hair pulled into a smooth bun at the nape of her neck. She wore a pair of shiny mirrored sunglasses on her face, out of place with the rugged practicality of the rest of the ranger uniform. The new ranger smiled. "Didn't mean to startle you, there. Everything okay?"

"Not really," Becca said truthfully.

Eitan elbowed her. "Can you tell us how to get back to the trail that leads up to the dam?"

"Without turning into evil Mr. Fantastic," Becca muttered, fussing with her maps to get them to sit properly back in their tube. Eitan elbowed her again.

"Evil Mr. Fantastic?" the ranger said, laughing a little. Naomi was slightly surprised she had heard them. "Sounds like there's a story there." She stepped closer. Naomi tasted pennies.

"We just had a, um, weird encounter," Naomi said carefully, scratching at her arms and shuffling her friends backward away from the ranger.

Either Becca was just more used to feeling strange in her own skin, or she was too preoccupied with her maps to notice that there was something weird about this ranger, too, because she didn't seem worried about the way the ranger was taking slow steps toward them. "Some monster park ranger tried to eat us, and her arms went all the way out to there!" Becca cried, throwing her arms wide.

"Oh my!" the ranger said. "How far?" She reached out. Her smile grew wider and wider, and her arms creaked and popped as they stretched way past their natural length and kept reaching for the kids. "This far?" she asked conversationally. She inhaled deeply through her nose. "You kids smell like magic."

They ran.

Once again, they ended up in the clearing with the strange, twisted stump. They barely had a moment to catch their breath before another ranger—this one a stout, cheerful-looking woman with a messy ponytail hanging over her shoulder—stepped out of the trees. Her eyes were deep pools of solid black, and she was already reaching for them with both arms. "You kids lost?" The voice didn't seem to come from her at all. It echoed around the clearing like it was a cave. Like the last woman, she sniffed the air and smiled. "Oh dear, what are you mixed up in? No wonder you were so easy to snare." She stepped forward. They stepped back, reaching out for one another. "Magic is as magic does. Let's see, now."

Becca bared her teeth and hissed at the demon like a mongoose. The woman stopped, something like confusion flickering across her face, and then she started to laugh. Eitan grabbed Becca and Naomi by the backs of their sweatshirts and hauled them out of the clearing. They could hear the woman's laughter echoing behind them as they ran.

This time Becca stopped them well before Naomi herself would have chosen to stop running. "What are you doing?" she demanded. "That thing is coming!"

"Wait," Becca said. "We're stuck in a loop. I think I've figured it out. The demon, or demons, whatever, they only ever show up in that clearing, right? And we keep ending up back there when-ever we run."

"I bet they're, like, feeding on our fear or some-thing," Naomi muttered.

"Actually—" Eitan started.

Becca made a frustrated noise. "Shut up. Listen. That clearing isn't on any of my maps. We're being herded back around to it over and over again, but the rest of the trails *are* on the map and seem like they should be going in straight lines." She stepped back into a small gap in the trees off the trail and beckoned them over. "Look." She traced the lines of the trails she was pointing at. "Now, we're here, see? But the clearing isn't anywhere on the map. It doesn't actually exist. We're getting looped in somewhere." Eitan and Naomi leaned over Becca's shoulder as she ran her fingers over the crisscrossing paths. "Here," she determined, jabbing at a spot that looked, to Naomi, like any other. "That's where we're losing the trail. We need to find that spot."

Naomi looked at Eitan, and they both nodded. Becca knew maps. Eitan punched her lightly in the shoulder. "All right. Lead the way, Becks."

. . .

All the trails looked pretty much like one another, but Naomi tried to see what Becca was seeing. She stuck close behind her friend, with Eitan close behind her, as Becca held her map up and muttered to herself every few steps. Eventually, they reached the turn that Becca insisted wasn't a real turn. It looked real. There was a large tree—so big that the three of them together probably wouldn't be able to wrap their arms around it—and a sharp drop-off into a ditch full of thistles that forced the trail to swerve off to the right. Naomi couldn't see how the trail could possibly go another way.

Becca stopped moving.

"What now?" Eitan asked.

"Look." Becca held out her map so they could see. "We're here, on this trail, at this trail marker. It's supposed to go straight, not curve off to the side."

"What, that way?" Naomi said, eyeing the big tree doubtfully. "There's no way to go that way."

Becca bit her lip. She was thinking, and thinking hard, based on the way her face was scrunched up. Becca's face always scrunched up when she was doing her best thinking. Then she sighed and drooped like a puppet with all its strings cut. "I don't really know," she admitted. "I'm just really sure that we shouldn't be going that way."

"What are our other options, Becks?" Naomi asked. "It's not like we can just go through the tree." Becca nodded glumly and chewed her lip some more. Naomi was just about to suggest that they find their way back to the campgrounds and start over when Becca's head snapped up.

"What?" Eitan asked.

"We go through the tree!" Becca said.

Naomi and Eitan stared at her. Finally, Eitan said, "Um . . . Becks?"

"No, no, I know, but listen. This turn isn't supposed to exist. It's supposed to go straight. That means that all the things that are keeping it from going straight are *also* not supposed to exist. Get it?"

"No," Eitan said.

"Wait." Naomi held up her hand. "You're saying that you don't think that ginormous tree surrounded by bramble bushes and a steep drop is actually there."

"Right," Becca said, like that wasn't completely ludicrous. "Think about it—the trees around here don't get that big. It's wrong." She said it like that was all there was to it. The tree was wrong; therefore, she was right, and they could carry on like it didn't exist.

"Sure," Naomi said faintly. "And you want us to just . . . walk through it."

Eitan walked over and put his hand on the tree, then knocked on it a few times. It made a solid *thunk* when his fist hit the bark. "*How?*" he asked.

Becca let out a shaky breath but didn't back down. "You're the one who keeps talking about magic. I'm telling you this tree doesn't exist. I'm not sure why that's harder to believe than the fact that demons do exist."

"Well," Eitan said, "for one thing, I can see the demons, and I can also *absolutely see this tree.*"

Becca set her jaw. "Do you trust me?"

"Yes," Naomi said immediately. She elbowed Eitan, who cleared his throat loudly.

"Erm, yes, obviously, Becks."

Becca nodded sharply. Then she rolled up her maps and put them back into the tube. "Good. Then you can hold these." She held the tube out to Eitan, who blinked at her.

"You want me to hold your maps?"

"That's why I'm handing them to you."

Eitan blinked some more. "But you never let me hold your maps. Last week you said that you would rather let Benji take your maps to show-and-tell than trust me to hold them."

Becca scowled at him. "Eitan. Take the frickin' maps." Eitan took the maps. He held them like he had been handed priceless jewels and carefully strapped the tube to his backpack. Naomi tried very hard not to smile too big at the way he was blushing at the gesture of trust. Becca could be full of surprises sometimes. "Okay," Becca said, "now line up behind me."

Naomi stepped into line behind Eitan as Becca stepped in front of him and turned to face the tree. "Close your eyes," she said.

"What?"

"Trust me," she repeated. They shut their eyes. "Okay, good, now put your hands on my shoulders, Eitan. Nae, hold on to his backpack. Follow me. Baby steps, okay? Just move when I move." She started to take slow, shuffling steps forward, and they moved. After about ten steps, Becca gasped sharply.

"Becks?" Naomi hissed.

"Keep your eyes shut!" Becca snapped. Naomi squeezed her eyelids tight, and Becca kept pulling them forward. Eitan made a short noise of surprise in front of her, then Naomi felt something rough and dry scrape against her skin. It was hard not to flinch. Naomi had run into a tree while riding her bike a few months earlier, and the bark had not been forgiving. It was hard to believe that walking face-first into this tree wouldn't also leave her skin raw and bleeding. She braced herself, wanting to open her eyes, but in the last couple of weeks, she had learned the hard way that her eyes couldn't always be trusted. Becca, though—Becca saw the world exactly as it was. Becca had always been very clear on what was true and right, and what wasn't. Naomi didn't trust her own eyes, but she trusted Becca to see what was real. She kept her eyes shut.

There was a strange moment when the air seemed to stretch and push against her eardrums. Naomi was cold, like the sun had suddenly disappeared behind thick clouds. The metallic taste was back, and it felt like she was wading through a thick, soupy liquid. Then Eitan gasped and stumbled forward, and Naomi's ears popped painfully. Ahead of her, Becca let out a shaky laugh. "Okay, you can open your eyes."

Naomi did, and let out a gasp of her own. They were standing on a wide trail that stretched out clear and straight in front of them. The sun slanted down toward them from the other side of the sky, harsh and too-bright like it got when it was close to sunset. She spun around, and the tree that had blocked the way was nowhere to be seen; neither were the tangle of brambles or the drop-off into the ditch. The heaviness in the air was dissipating slowly, and the goose bumps on Naomi's arms were fading. She took a deep breath of the newly clean air. Eitan let out a whoop and swept Becca off her feet into a spinning hug. She growled and swatted at him until he dropped her and he swept Naomi up instead.

"You did it, Becks!" he shouted. "That was amazing! I will literally never underestimate your maps ever again. Oh my God." Naomi laughed and wriggled away from him. She held her fist out, and Becca tapped her own against it with a small smile.

"I can't believe that worked," she said quietly.

Naomi grinned. "I can." Becca ducked her

head, looking pleased, but before Naomi could say anything else, an echoing crash rang out through the woods and made the ground beneath them tremble. All three of them froze.

"You don't think . . . ," Eitan started, staring in the direction of the noise.

Naomi swallowed. "Yeah," she said. "I do."

Becca patted her on the shoulder. "Come on," she said. "Let's go save the world."

17

ABANDONING THE WORK

After everything they had dealt with—ghosts, a dybbuk, biking more miles than Naomi even wanted to think about, and finally the ordeal with the demons and the trail loop—the way up to the lake area felt surprisingly short. The bushes grew thinner and more scrubby around them, and the trails flattened out to cross over flat drives and wider dirt roads. The ground continued to shake, the tremors getting stronger as they went. Every reverberating crash made the kids wince and stumble as they hurried up the trail, growing louder as they got closer, until it was nearly deafening. The trail finally spit them out onto a wide bank dotted with picnic tables and scrubby trees. Naomi took a moment to be grateful that it was winter, which meant there was no one up at the lake.

The lake itself stretched out in front of them toward the dam, which rose in an oddly uniform hill of perfectly packed earth between the lower and upper lakes. Roads crisscrossed over it, and Naomi could see cars abandoned all along the shoulder. She hoped the people who had been in them were safe. The Golem was in the lower lake, methodically pulling chunks of earth from a gaping hole in the smooth wash of the dam. Rubble clouded the water behind him, and the concrete core of the dam was visible in the hole the Golem had created, but none of that was what made the kids stop in their tracks. The Golem was *enormous*. He towered over the lake, easily reaching the height of some of the trees on the surrounding trails. When he walked, the ground shook, and the water around his legs churned and rippled out in foot-high waves. Naomi stared, feeling tears well up in her eyes. This was so much worse than she had thought.

Distantly, she heard sirens beginning to wail. That made sense. The Golem had definitely been noticed, and Naomi was sure that there had to be sensors on the dam to stop things like this from happening. It didn't matter. Whoever was coming with the sirens, Naomi knew, would be too little too late. The Golem was moving fast, and she didn't think for a second that a few police officers would be enough to make him abandon a task. "He's trying to dig a hole through the dam," she whispered. "How do we stop this?" She felt Eitan's hand slip into hers as he stepped up beside her.

"I don't know," he said, "but you have to. The cops are coming. Why is he doing this?"

On Naomi's other side, Becca took a breath. "I know it's probably not what you want to hear, but this dam is where the western part of the California aqueduct ends. It's the drinking water for western Los Angeles. If he gets through, it's going to be a serious problem for a lot of people."

"But *why* is he doing it?" Eitan asked again.

"Protecting the wilderness," Naomi realized, horror making her stomach twist in knots. "He's trying to get rid of the people so the environment can come back."

"That's not how it works!" Eitan protested.

"Well, I don't think he's got a super-great understanding of environmental science, Eitan," Naomi snapped. "We never bothered to teach him that."

"But holy heck, Nae, this isn't what we meant. It's not what we wanted."

"I know," Naomi cried. "He's got it all mixed up. All the stuff we told him, they're human problems. There are ways for humans to fix them, and that's what we thought we were telling him. He's trying to help, but he's not human. He can't fix it."

"It doesn't matter why he's doing it," Becca said. "*Look at him.* We gave him a task, and he's doing it the way he thinks he should, and he's going to keep doing it. It doesn't matter if that's what we meant. We have to do something *now*."

"We have to do something now," Naomi repeated. "We're here. We have a responsibility." She laughed a little to herself and made a face. "Fine, okay, I get it. Human solutions. Responsibility. I get it," she repeated. "Okay, Rabbi Gershon, 'hineni.'"

Her friends looked at her like she'd gone a little

crazy. "Oh-*kay*," Becca said. "But what does that *mean*, Nae?"

Naomi met Becca's eyes. "It means that Rabbi Gershon told us how to stop him." She darted in and grabbed Becca in a quick hug, which surprised her friend so much she actually hugged back. Then she turned and wrapped her arms around Eitan, who was far more prepared for it and squeezed her back tightly for a long moment. "I love you guys," she said. "Stay here."

Naomi took off running toward the Golem, ignoring the questioning protests of her friends behind her. She got as close to the Golem as she could on land, and then she waded out into the shallows. She didn't dare go barefoot with all the rubble covering the bottom of the lake, and the water soaked through her tennis shoes and made her feet feel like weights. Her jeans, too, were heavy and cold against her legs. It was freezing, despite the bright sunshine, and Naomi gasped as her legs began to tingle with the cold. It made the crisp, California winter air around her feel warm and heavy in comparison. Naomi plunged forward, fighting all the instincts that screamed at her to get out of the water and get warm. She got up to her waist in the water before she stopped. She still wasn't close enough to touch him, but the Golem had always seemed to hear her before. She sucked in a huge breath of air and shouted at the top of her lungs, "*Golem!*" The Golem seemed to regard her curiously for a moment, but he didn't slow. Naomi tried again. "Golem! Stop!"

The Golem did slow that time. He seemed confused. There was a strange tension in his clay limbs, like he was fighting two separate instincts and wasn't sure which to follow. "Stop!" Naomi said again. "Stop, please. You're not obligated!" The shape of the word felt strange on her tongue, but it was the right one. Naomi knew it. A large piece of rock crumbled off the dam and crashed into the water near her, causing a wave that crested over her head and soaked her. Naomi screamed and scrambled to keep her footing, but the wave was too strong.

Water closed over her head, and she tumbled over, the wave sweeping her into the deeper part of the lake. The weak winter sun couldn't reach through the dirt and debris in the water, and Naomi floundered in the dark. She kicked with her legs until her feet hit the ground again and she pushed up, hard. Her head broke the surface.

The big rock was still close by, and she splashed her way toward it until she could cling to the uneven side of it, coughing around the water in her mouth and shaking out her hair so she could see. She needed to be up higher, or this wasn't going to work.

Naomi scrambled up the chunk of earth and concrete, feeling the rough edges of it cut into her hands. The Golem turned to watch her with thunderous steps, a giant boulder braced precariously in his hand. Naomi stood up shakily and steadied herself on the rock as it shook beneath her with the Golem's steps. When it stilled again, she took a deep breath and said in the most commanding voice she could muster—one that would give her mom's lawyer voice a run for its money—"This is not your work!"

The Golem tilted his head, the boulder in his hand wobbling dangerously. Naomi dropped flat against her rock as the boulder fell and sent another wave crashing over everything, but her fingers missed the edge and she was swept back into the water. She could hear Eitan and Becca shouting behind her before she went under. She was sure, this time, that she was going to drown.

It was too cold and too dark. Her clothes were heavy, and her arms and legs felt heavier. Then a large, earthen hand plunged into the water and closed around her. Naomi screamed as she was lifted into the air. The Golem brought her to his eye level and then fell still—his usual waiting pose—with that uncertain tension vibrating through him like a plucked guitar string. Naomi coughed again, trying to clear out her lungs enough to shout. She pounded on the Golem's huge fingers with her fists. "This is not your work! You didn't choose this path! You are not obligated to complete it!" Several long, terrifying seconds passed, and then all at once the Golem moved.

She didn't even have time to scream again before the Golem shifted its stiff, giant body and began walking toward Eitan and Becca on the bank. The water churned beneath them with each step, and Naomi realized that the choppy surface of the lake was getting closer. The Golem was shrinking. He got smaller and smaller as they walked across the lake, giving her the strange sense of falling in slow motion. By the time they reached the bank, he was about the size of her mama and was holding her in a fireman's carry

Her tears dropped into the dirt below them, a few more drops of water in the already soaked bank of the lake. "Okay," she said. Slowly, she reached up to the nearly invisible seam in the Golem's head and pried it open. As soon as her fingers closed around the scroll, she felt the change. The sunbaked warmth of the Golem's clay faded away until it was nothing but cool earth. All the fine details of the Golem's face seemed to blur. Naomi pulled the scroll from its head and stepped back. Almost in slow motion, the Golem crumbled. When it was over, there was nothing but a pile of fine red clay left on the ground. Naomi held the scroll in her hand.

"You're supposed to bury it," Eitan whispered. Naomi looked up at him. "You know," he went on quietly, "like you do with an old prayerbook. I'm pretty sure it counts as a holy text." Naomi looked at the scroll. What Eitan said felt right. Even if it wasn't a holy text, it was basically the Golem's soul. It deserved a proper burial, and to be with the rest of the Golem.

She knelt beside the pile of clay and dug a small hole through the center of the pile and down into the wet dirt of the riverbank. She

18

A MYSTERIOUS PACKAGE, AGAIN

They made it halfway back down the hill before Eitan stopped and rounded on Naomi. All his earlier seriousness had been replaced with normal almost-thirteen-year-old righteous fury. "You are completely insane!" he yelled. "I cannot *believe* you did that. That was the craziest thing I have ever seen anyone do, and if I weren't so relieved that you aren't dead, I would *literally* kill you!" He stopped, breathing hard, and then burst into tears. Becca snorted, but she was looking distinctly teary herself.

"Eitan." Naomi took a step toward him, and he held up a hand.

"You can't hug me like that, Nae. You're drip-ping wet. Here." He pulled his sweatshirt over his head, leaving him in his long-sleeved Camp Ramah T-shirt. "I'll close my eyes." Naomi took the sweatshirt gratefully. She stepped behind a nearby tree and stripped out of her wet layers, trading them for the warm, dry fleece while Becca stood guard against anyone who might see.

"All clear," she announced when she was dressed. "Thanks, Eitan." He let out another choked sob, and then he was hugging her tightly. Naomi leaned into it gratefully, laughing a little when Becca scooted in and hooked her chin over Naomi's shoulder.

"I'm not giving you my pants," Becca said. Naomi laughed for real then and pulled back, blinking away her tears.

"I wouldn't expect you to, Becks. I did the crazy thing; I have to live with the chafing."

Eitan nodded. "Damn straight."

He grinned at Becca's mocking gasp of "*Language*, Eitan!"

"What can I say, Becks. I'm a rebel." He stopped smiling and put his hands on Naomi's shoulders. "Seriously, though, Nae. I am so proud of you." He also made her a bunch of her special matzah ball soup with chicken, and none of their parents suspected the three of them had had anything to do with the mess at the dam. They had coordinated their stories at the campground while they waited for Eitan's dad to come get them. In the end, they had gone with the geocaching story, since it seemed as plausible as anything else. They told their parents that Troy—who Eitan's parents already didn't like—had set up a race to a cache full of cool stuff his mom had brought back from business trips abroad and that telling any parents would have disqualified them. Naomi was shocked that her parents believed it, but she supposed there wasn't really an obvious reason to lie.

Being grounded was okay. Naomi had to go back to school the day after they got back from the dam, so it wasn't like she was home all day, though she didn't think she would have minded either way. She did her homework and practiced her prayers, but the rest of the time she wasn't feeling up for much besides lying in bed and sitting with her mom while she caught up on cases. Mom kept asking if she wanted to talk, but Naomi didn't know what she would say. She had stopped feeling the strange aura that appeared whenever something magical was around. There was no sense of someone watching her through the sliding glass door, no weird encounters at the grocery store, no more goose bumps or chittering voices or whispering ghosts at the temple. She tried to feel relieved by that, but mostly she felt sad. The magic disappearing was one more sign that the Golem was really gone, and she didn't think she could explain that in a way her moms would understand. Instead, she stole her mama's softest sweaters, ate her soup, and cried in her room when she could call Eitan and Becca, who did understand. She also spent a lot of time rewriting her Bat Mitzvah speech. Rabbi Levinson had seemed surprised that Naomi wanted to rewrite the speech she had spent so long on, but Naomi had to. She sent him the final copy two days before her Bat Mitzvah, and his reply had just said: *Wow.*

"It's a scary thought," Naomi said, looking out over the assembled congregation. "It's *hard*. We do everything we can to change the world for the better. We listen for those moments where we can say 'hineni.' We choose the righteous path when we can, we take responsibility when we need to, and it still feels like nothing changes. We're so small when you think about the size of the world and its troubles."

Naomi looked at Eitan's bright grin in the front row of the synagogue. Becca beside him was trying to look grumpy and failing, her smile peeking through at the corners. Naomi returned their smiles and turned back to the microphone. "Who are we that God should demand such works from us?" She shrugged. "Then again, who was Moses? Did Moses save the world, or did he save his corner of it? Are we angry at him that he didn't do enough? If you save the part of the world that's yours, haven't *you* done enough? Recently, someone very wise told me a saying. He said 'We are not obligated to complete the work, but neither are we free to abandon it.'"

Naomi looked down at the rich, polished wood of the podium, red cherrywood the color of fired clay. "For the people who want to help, the important part is that we are not obligated to complete the work. Some people forget this, and it makes them sad or even angry. It makes them blame others for taking breaks. It makes it harder for them to keep working, because they never see that things are getting better. So what do we do? The answer is: what we can. Every day, we do what we can. We offer help to people who need it, we give the pieces of ourselves that we can spare, but if we let ourselves feel responsible for everything that's wrong in the world, we won't ever feel strong enough to take action. If we focus on how much sadness there is, we'll be too busy dealing with the grief to hear that moment when we're called to action. God doesn't send burning bushes anymore. God isn't going to text us or send an angel to tell us to stop and go back down the mountain. It's our job, as people, to notice the moments when it's our time to say 'hineni.' It's our job to try. *That's* how we save the world."

Later, after Rabbi Levinson finished the blessings, and Naomi's moms hugged her and cried, and Deena gave her a little shake and said, "You did good, munchkin," and Eitan and Becca pulled her into an empty classroom so they could have another, mostly happy cry, there was a party. Naomi had a dress that sparkled when she twirled, and her mom had paid a hairdresser to make her curls do something fashionable for once. They danced, and they ate too much dessert, and a lot of the grown-ups, in her mama's words, "took advantage of the open bar."

There was also a table of presents that Naomi was dying to open. Most of them were envelopes with practical things like savings bonds and checks written out in multiples of eighteen, but there were a few boxes. Naomi grabbed another cookie from the buffet and drifted over to the gift table, just to see what was there. Eitan and Becca caught up with her, Becca looking disgruntled and Eitan breathless and flushed from dancing. Eitan's tie was crooked, and Becca had abandoned her shoes an hour ago. Naomi grinned at them.

"We made it."

"Heck yeah we did," Eitan said, holding out his hand for a high five, "and now you get the presents!"

"So many presents," Becca said, eyeing the table longingly. "Only two more weeks until it's my turn!"

Naomi laughed. "You're going to do great."

"Duh," Becca said, "though there's really no following that speech of yours."

Naomi opened her mouth to reply; then her eyes caught on one of the presents, and she forgot what she was going to say.

"Nae?" Eitan nudged her with his elbow. "You good?"

She pointed wordlessly at the perfectly square package wrapped in reddish-brown paper. Eitan gasped, and Becca said a word low under her breath that Naomi was inclined to agree with. She snatched it off the table and pulled her friends into the hall and behind a pillar. They huddled together as she opened it, Eitan making sure to block the view of anyone who came out the doors after them. The paper came off easily when Naomi pulled at it, revealing the plain white box with a nearly invisible seam around the top. It was the same weird material as before, not cardboard or ceramic but something Naomi couldn't identify. The lid slid off without much pressure from her, revealing a little clay figure, the same reddish brown of the wrapping paper, resting in a nest of soft packaging. There was a tightly rolled scroll resting on top of the tissue paper held closed with a silver wax seal. Naomi dug her nails into it and yanked it open. Across the top, in neat, typewritten text, it said: *For Naomi. Just in case.* Pins and needles raced up her arms.

The three of them stared at one another with wide eyes. "*Who?*" Becca demanded. "Nae, this is insane. We can't just accept that someone out there wants you to have magic and not try to find them."

Naomi shook her head. "We don't need to find them. It doesn't matter."

"It doesn't?" Eitan asked disbelievingly.

"No," Naomi said firmly. "It doesn't." She put the clay figurine and its note into her dress pocket and tipped the box into the trash. "I don't know who's sending me these, or why. Maybe they've been sending them to a bunch of people, and we were just the only ones who woke theirs up. Maybe there's only one and someone is trying to get me in trouble. I don't care. We're not doing this again." She looked up and met her friends' incredulous looks. "We'll bury him in the backyard. A proper send-off. But we won't wake him up. We tried it that way," she said. "We tried to make it all someone else's problem. We're done doing that."

Behind them, the music switched over to something familiar and loud. Naomi heard the cheers of her friends and classmates in the hall. "Human solutions for human problems. We're going to save the world on our own, you guys." She grinned at her friends. "But first Becca has to dance." Becca spluttered, and Naomi, laughing, pulled her friends back into the party.

ACKNOWLEDGMENTS

Thank you to everyone who picked up a copy of this book and chose to share this adventure with Naomi. I'm so grateful you're here.

And to the people I wouldn't be here without: Thank you to Miranda for always holding me to the best version of my work, and for refusing to accept my imposter syndrome.

Thank you to Stephanie, my agent, and Reka, my editor, for loving Naomi as much as I do, and for believing in me and the story I wanted to tell. I really don't have the words to express how grateful I am to both of you for your guidance and faith.

Thank you to Ariela for knowing more about L.A. and geography than I ever will. Without you, those poor kids would still be riding their bikes in circles in The Valley. Thank you, Talia, for taking the time out of your busy pre-med schedule to offer me insights. And thank you, Brianna, for your sage advice and your motivational s'mores.

Finally, a huge thank-you to Rabbi Nat for letting me bug you about Jewish folklore on your coffee break, and for lending me the book that started it all.

SAMARA SHANKER has been making up stories about magic and monsters since she was a kid sneaking in extra reading past her bedtime. By graduate school, she had moved on to writing stories that reimagined the folklore and mythology she had always loved as a kid (mostly still written after bedtime, once she finished all her sensible homework). She works now as a tutor and children's literacy specialist, and gets to do most of her writing during the day, which has done wonders for her sleep schedule. She lives in Virginia with her rescue puppy, Jack Kirby, and devotes most of her time not spent working or writing to spoiling her niece and nephew. This is her debut novel.